The Girl Who Knew Death

by

Norm Harris

The Girl Who Knew Death

Cover Art by *Diana Carlile*

The Wild Rose Press, Inc.
PO Box 708
Adams Basin, NY 14410-0708
Visit us at www.thewildrosepress.com

Publishing History
First Edition, 2022
Trade Paperback ISBN 978-1-5092-4231-3
Digital ISBN 978-1-5092-4232-0

Published in the United States of America

The tourist dressed in white shorts and running shoes, a tangerine top, a ball cap, sunglasses, and a red backpack descended the gang plank from the ship to the dock at Cruise Ships Dock at Limassol, New Port. Once on the dock, she paused to ensure the two men lurking in the shadows of the terminal building had noticed her. She hailed a cab. Her destination was the Russian Embassy in the nearby capitol of Nicosia.

The trip to the embassy would take almost two hours. Occasionally, she checked to be sure the men were keeping up with her. She wanted to know where they were at all times. Each morning, she began her day with but one simple rule Irishka has once taught her: "Every morning in Africa, a gazelle wakes up. It knows it must run faster than the fastest lion or it will be killed. Every morning, a lion wakes up. It knows it must outrun the slowest gazelle or it will starve to death. It doesn't matter whether you're a lion or gazelle. When the sun comes up, you'd better be running." *I must run today. Every day. Without fail*, Kat thought.

Praise for Norm Harris

"…a smart, believable suspense-filled mystery. Military enthusiasts will find Norm Harris's penchant for accuracy refreshing."

~ Cal Glomstad, former CBS News reporter, CTE/Contemporary World Issues/Instructor, WYA- Washington State Military Department.

"Norm Harris's book grabs the reader with its first sentence and holds the reader throughout with its fast-paced action. Dialogue is always the hardest to write, but Harris has captured the art and with his writing keeps the reader turning pages, his ability to heighten the intrigue keeps the reader on the edge of his or her seat throughout the story. Strongly recommend the book."

~ CAPT David E. Meadows, US Navy, author of numerous military thrillers such as Sixth Fleet, Seawolf, and Tomcat.

Dedication

For my son, Kristopher-Kent Herbert Harris, with love and amazement.

IN MEMORY
Josephine Hindman, Gladys Richardson, Nell Gelis, Eunice Harris, and Jack Brix.

Acknowledgments

Many thanks to those friends and associates who made this book happen, be it for your technical advice, editing, proofreading, or simply moral support: Jeanette Lundgren Navy Captain David Meadows, Carolyn Starr, Alexis Singletary "Attorney at Law", and Sheriff Jack Gardner. A special thank you goes out to Kathleen Jackson, and Mom and Dad. Thank you all for both your inspiration and valued friendships.

A special thank you to Carolyn Shafer for her superb edit and proofreading.

Prologue

Cairo, Egypt, 3:00 A.M.

A full moon rose from the east across the Nile. The morning's soft desert breeze was pleasantly warm. The businessman lit a second cigarette as he stood bathed in the moon's glow. A great white raven watched with interest from a nearby date palm as a woman softly slipped up behind the man. He was not aware of her presence – at least not until he likely felt the first of three quick jabs as the woman's knife was plunged repeatedly into his right side. He fell over the railing and into the Nile. The raven cawed one time. She spread her wings and took flight.

Chapter 1

"The news is unfortunate, Faya," Sasha said. "It is time I most dreaded. The Grand Duchess has died."

"How sad," Fay commiserated. "And you are right. The time has come. Katrinka must decide her future."

"The Grand Duchess's son, Prince Eugen, declined headship," Sasha informed Fay. "It means the headship passes to the next in line. It may well be Katrinka."

"This presents multiple problems for us," Fay added.

"Katrinka is now twenty-five. She has worked hard to put her life as a sparrow and as an espionage agent behind her."

Fay said, "She has a job in a coffee shop near the university and she is completing her first year at the medical school. She is near to her dream of becoming a nurse. And she is dancing. You know it all, Sasha."

"She tells me she is happiest she has been in her life," Sasha went on. "She has a man of interest, her cat, a job, and her study at university."

"So, what do we do, my dear friend?" Fay asked. "Tell her she is a princess who may one day be the Grand Duchess of Russia? Or not tell her and let her happy life play itself out here in America? She is very fond of her boyfriend. She can become a mother to little soccer-playing children. She dreams of a home and a good husband."

"There is another problem," Sasha said with a sigh. "I have contact in Kremlin who tells me the Grand Duchess named Katrinka in her will. She will assume the title of Lady Katrinka."

"You are referring to a sizeable inheritance, Sasha," Fay realized.

"She would not receive all," Sasha clarified. "Prince Eugen was left the bulk. Katrinka's share is maybe only ninety million plus U.S."

"Imagine, Sasha, what the money alone would do to her simple happy life!" Fay exclaimed. "How would any twenty-five-year-old deal with this?"

"Your life will change, Faya. My life will change. The rest of our lives will be devoted to advising and protecting her from any and all." Sasha sighed. "Are you ready to live your life wherever Katrinka so chooses?"

Fay laughed. "At least she would have two good lawyers for advisors, right!?"

"That she would!" Sasha said in a spirited voice.

"Can we agree to take some time to discuss this? You are not getting any pressure on this, are you?" Fay asked.

"Prince Eugen's family is not aware of Katrinka's whereabouts," Sasha told Fay. "Or if she is even alive. The Russian government knows she is with you in America. At this time, they do not seem interested. But their temperament could change quickly. There is talk in Russia the people want a unitary state with devolution, which is governed within the framework of a parliamentary democracy under a constitutional monarchy."

"The monarch, presumably Katrinka," Fay

continued, "would be the head of state while President Rudkovsky would remain the political leader. Is it possible, Sasha?"

"It was not too long ago our country moved from communism to a federal democratic state. The title of Grand Duchess as a symbol of old Russia may change," he replied. "I don't know."

"I lived eight years as a First Daughter," Fay reminded Sasha. "But I cannot begin to fathom what this life would be for Katrinka. She would lose all hope of living a normal life as a wife and mother."

"I know it, Faya," Sasha acknowledged. "My heart is heavy. There is third option. We will tell Katrinka. We are her trusted advisors. We will explain to her what her life would become should she choose to be Grand Duchess of Russia or happy soccer mom of United States. Which would you choose, Faya?"

"There is but one answer. I believe we should tell her and let her decide," Fay concluded.

"I fear if we do not tell her and should she find out later, we will lose the trust she has in us," Sasha agreed.

"You are right, of course," Fay said. "How and when do we tell her?"

"You, I, and Irishka would plan to meet at a time when we are all three able. New York, LA, Moscow…?" Sasha suggested.

"Have you spoken to Irishka?" Fay inquired.

"Irishka believes we should tell her," Sasha said.

"Irishka's life changes as well."

"Irishka is military," Sasha replied. "She is also a pragmatic woman. Because she is military, she understands her life choices are not her own. When it was discovered Katrinka was descendant of the last

Tsar, Russian military assigned Irishka to protect her. Because Katrinka had spy school training, Irishka thought it best for Katrinka to be brought into Russian military intelligence with her. Katrinka excelled as Irishka's protegee. They are like sisters."

"There is so much that is Katrinka," Fay stated. "I can't even begin to understand how complex her life has been already."

"I suppose I am more aware of it. Russian military is not same as American military," Sasha explained. "Katrinka was trained at the Foreign Intelligence Service, *Sluzhba Vneshney Razvedk Academy* in Moscow. We call 'The Institute.' She was taught English, counterintelligence and investigation. She had begun Federal Security Service Institute of Computer Science. But she withdrew."

"I appreciate your explaining this to me," Fay said. "I don't speak of the past with Katrinka, only of the present and the future."

"I had difficult time convincing U.S. embassy in Moscow to grant visa allowing Katrinka to relocate to U.S."

"Good job, Sasha!" Fay praised.

"There are those in Russia who welcome a move toward a form of constitutional monarchy," Sasha told her, "others for the systems to remain as they are. And others are moving to return Russia to a communistic state. Those who represent the monarchy would be caught in the political crossfire. It has the potential for a dangerous situation."

****

Sofitel Hotel, four weeks later, Cairo, Egypt
They met in Fay and Katrinka's room. Sasha spoke

to Kat in her native language. He reasoned she would better digest the complexity of the meeting in her native language. Because Fay did not understand Russian, she relied on body language, as she would if she were in a courtroom. Sasha spoke in a soft and caring tone. Katrinka did not speak, only intently listened. Her obedient eyes never left his. Fay had seldom seen Irishka smile. During this discussion, her smile was constant. Irishka's smile conveyed confidence and encouragement to Kat.

In Russian, Sasha told Katrinka, "Your family and friends are with you today to tell you about your past life which you do not yet know. And we want you to know about your real family. Irishka, Faya, and me want you to know that what comes of this and what your decisions will be that we are and will always be at your side."

Fay had only experienced the happy side of Kat, the Kat who always smiled and had an unrelenting positive attitude. She had yet to know the angry or depressed side of Katrinka. In Fay's mind, these were moods Katrinka was not capable of. And she had never seen Katrinka cry. Yet, from the onset, Katrinka had sensed this meeting may not have a happy outcome for her. Katrinka's eyes immediately flooded with tears.

Irishka said something to Kat. Fay assumed it to be words of reassurance because Irishka drew a smile from Katrinka's lips, accompanied by a hopeful nod.

Sasha continued speaking in Russian. "This will be good. I want you to be courageous and brave girl I know as Katrinka."

Kat nodded and said, "I will, Papa."

"Because of political climate in Russia at the time

of your birth, your mother, Sofia Romanova, had to flee Russia. Do you know the name of family Romanov?" Sasha asked Kat.

Katrinka replied, "Romanoff?"

"Yes, my dear, last tsar of Russia."

"I do not understand, Papa," Kat said, "it is me?"

"Be patient. I will tell you all," Sasha assured her.

Katrinka replied with an obedient nod.

Sasha began the story of a life Katrinka did not know. "Your mother trusted the man and his wife who you knew as your mother and father, who was Russian army General Yuri Markov, and, of course, your mother Martina Markova," he told Kat. "They were to care for you until your mother could find a way to come back to you. Before your mother could return, she became ill. As time moved on, political climate in Russia changed again and Yuri lost all of his pension. you gave up everything at age thirteen to earn money in order to support your parents."

Fay's life had had its fair share of sadness but the emotion that now claimed her heart was at its apex.

"You did what you must do and you should always feel pride in how you have managed your life to this day." Sasha paused to seemingly allow Katrinka time to let this sink in.

Sasha continued. "You know when you were nineteen years, Irishka met you and helped you to join Russian military."

Katrinka nodded and acknowledged Irishka with a thankful nod and a smile.

"You proved to be an exceptional student," Sasha continued. "As you know, it was short time later I met you."

"Thank you, Papa," Katrinka said.

"You met Faya and now we are here today," Sasha finished.

Katrinka turned to Fay. With a look of deep appreciation etched in her face, she said in English, "Thank you, Faya."

"You now have decision to make." Sasha continued the conversation in English. "You are relative of Russian Grand Duchess Natalya Veriskaya. She recently died. Her son, and your uncle, Prince Eugen, is next for title but he does not want it. You are Lady Katrinka and may be asked to assume title of Princess Romanova."

Sasha paused again. Katrinka seemed to be taking the news very well but then again, Fay could not feel Katrinka's heart and soul.

Sasha asked, "Katrinka, what do you think about this?"

"I do not understand it, Papa," Kat answered. "What does it mean?"

"Faya will explain what it means for you," Sasha said.

Katrinka turned her attention to Fay.

In English, Fay explained, "What this will mean is you may be offered a choice. This is where you will choose the next road on which you will travel. But whatever road you choose, we three want you to know we are with you for better or for worse." Fay reached for Katrinka's hand. As she held Kat's hand, she asked, "Okay?"

Kat again nodded.

Kat turned to Irishka. She spoke in Russian.

Irishka replied.

Katrinka turned back to Fay. "Faya," she said, "Irishka say to me you are my voice. I will do as you say."

Fay looked at Irishka and smiled. Turning her attention back to Kat, Fay said, "This will be your decision. But you do have choices. If you decide to rejoin your family in Russia as Lady Katrinka, and one day Princess of Russia, your life will change in unexplainable ways. The life you now know in America will no longer exist. Your life will be as if you are a rock star or a celebrity, everyone will know your name, but it may not be a happy life. You will not ever be a nurse. What will become of Andrew and the life you may have dreamed of? You will have much money and much responsibility. You will have some power to change people's lives and you may make good changes for the people of Russia. So too our lives will forever change. Sasha, Irishka, and me will never leave you alone."

"You, and Papa, and Irishka will leave Navy to become my advisors?" Katrinka clarified.

"Yes, sweetie. Our lives will become your life," Fay reassured her.

"This is too much to know about," Katrinka mildly protested. "It is too much for me to think about. What is other option for me?"

Fay smiled. "There is second choice for you," she told the younger woman. "You can say no to it all and remain living in Bremerton or wherever you choose to live. You could grow old, become a babushka."

"I can think about this? I have all of you for best advice?" Katrinka asked.

"Of course," Fay said. "But there is one more

thing. The Grand Duchess put your name into her will. You know what a will is, don't you?"

"It is a dream someone has left big money for you?" Kat guessed.

"Yes. Not a dream, but yes," Fay responded. "The Grand Duchess wished for you to have ninety million U.S. dollars."

Katrinka's reaction to Fay's disclosure was a look of panic across her face. "I don't know what it is. I cannot believe it," Kat gasped. "I already have two hundred thousand U.S. Why do I need more? It is too much for me," she protested.

Fay tried to understand what Katrinka must be feeling. "Do not think about it right now. We will help you when the time comes," she promised.

"So, I can have life in Russia as super rich princess? And hope to make life better of all Russian people? Or I continue to live in U.S. and be happy wife and mother and nurse?" Kat summed up.

Fay was impressed by how quickly Katrinka had digested all that had been dumped on her and had quickly broken it down into two seemingly simple choices. Fay now reasoned it may have been quicker to simply ask Katrinka, "Do you want to be a Russian Princess? Or an American soccer mom?"

Katrinka's entire mood brightened. "This is good, I think?" she said. "It is better than I imagine. I thought at first you all were going to give me some kind of bad news."

Fay, Irishka, and Sasha laughed. This may have been the first time Fay had seen Irishka laugh. So, the Iron Spy woman did know laughter.

Fay said, "Bless your heart, sweetie, may you

remain forever young."

****

Midday, Sofitel Hotel, Cairo, Egypt

"They have big swimming pool!" Katrinka informed Fay. "This will be good! Only time I swim was in military school. I swim for two hours without stop, then someone tries to fight me. It is hard not to drowned."

Fay shook her head. Katrinka was a constant source of joy and wonder. Fay particularly enjoyed Kat's spy school stories. They were so matter of fact, as if everyone had attended a spy school during their formative years.

Katrinka left the room with the intent of meeting Irishka in the hotel lobby. The two would spend a few hours at the swimming pool.

At ten minutes past, Fay readied herself. She intended to meet Katrinka and Irishka at the pool. She heard a knock at the door. Fay opened the door. It was Irishka.

"I was to mcct Katrinka in lobby. Is shc hcrc?" Irishka asked.

"She left ten minutes ago to meet you," Fay informed her.

Alarms went off in both women's minds.

"We must rush to pool," Irishka said.

As the two women raced along the hallway leading to the pool, Fay managed to text Katrinka: *Where are you?*

The text was immediately returned: *I wait for Irishka in lobby.*

Shortly, the two women arrived at the lobby. Not able to spot Katrinka, Fay texted: *We are at lobby. We don't see you.*

No response.

A concerned Irishka said to Fay, "Find Sasha. I go to reception to know if anyone saw her in lobby."

Fay texted Sasha: *We cannot find Katrinka. Is she with you?*

She is not with you? Sasha texted in reply.

Fay frantically searched the lobby, while Irishka spoke to the man at reception. Both women then met back in the lobby.

Irishka reported, "Man says he saw Katrinka with two men. They appeared to be officials. Maybe Egyptian National Police?" she speculated.

"I found her cell phone on a chair," Fay revealed. She pointed in the direction of the chair. "I will contact the American Embassy here in Cairo. Hopefully they will advise us on how to deal with the local police."

"In case American Embassy no help, I will ask Sasha to contact Russian Embassy," Irishka added.

Sasha arrived in the lobby. Irishka informed him of their plan to contact the embassies. Sasha grew deeply concerned. "Faya, if Katrinka has been arrested by Egyptian police and should they learn of her former connection with Russian GRU, they may well execute her for spy. Same for Irishka. Both could be exposed. We must act fast."

Chapter 2

"Deputy Chief of Missions Adel McKinny from the American Embassy called me," Fay told Irishka and Sasha. "Rather than discuss this on the phone, she said she would clear her schedule and asked us to meet her this afternoon at the U.S. Embassy. When I travel abroad, habit is to pack my uniform," she told them. "Occasionally, I have found the uniform useful. I found doors which were initially closed have opened for a lady in a uniform."

Fay traveled to her meeting with Adel McKinny alone. She reasoned an introduction of the Russian spy, and suspected assassin, Irishka, to a U.S. Embassy Deputy Chief of Missions might be a dicey proposition. Sasha and Irishka, in the meantime, headed for the Russian Cairo Embassy.

Fay arrived at the U.S. Embassy shortly past 4 P.M. She paid the cab driver and proceeded toward the gate. One of the four Marines posted at the gate met her near the gate center.

"How may I help you, ma'am?" the Marine asked.

"Hello, Corporal," Fay returned her greeting. "I have a meeting with Missions Officer Adel McKinny."

"Thank you, ma'am. May I see your ID please?" the Corporal requested.

Fay presented her passport to the Corporal.

The other woman examined several pages and then

asked, "May I see your CAC, ma'am?"

Fay handed the Corporal her Command Access Card.

"One moment, ma'am, while I scan your card." After a brief moment, the Corporal returned. She handed Fay back her CAC and then snapped to attention, saluted, and spoke. "Welcome to the U.S. Embassy, Commander Green." She then opened one of the two gates, allowing Fay to enter the Embassy grounds.

As Fay passed through the gates, the Corporal barked, "Officer on deck!"

The remaining three guards snapped to attention and saluted.

Fay asked the Corporal, "Will you escort me to Mission Officer McKinny's office?"

Corporal Lopez said, "This way, ma'am," as she began walking toward the door.

"How has your day been, Corporal?" Fay inquired.

"Outstanding, ma'am. I mean it literally. It is freakin' hot out here. I am going to bless you for getting me out of the sun, if only for a moment," Lopez answered.

"Corporal, I am going to be with Mrs. McKinny for a while. Will you wait inside for me?" Fay requested. "I may need help finding my way back out of here."

"You bet I will, ma'am." Lopez seemed very happy. "We are going to the second floor, ma'am," she went on. "The elevator is slow. Do you mind taking the stairs?"

"No, I don't mind at all."

As the two women ascended the stairs, Lopez said, "I have met you before, ma'am."

Over the years, especially during her time spent living in the White House, it seemed Fay had met so many diplomats and celebrities, but she could not recall many of their faces or names.

"We did meet, Corporal." A statement, not a question. Fay was fishing for a time and place. "How have you been?" she asked. "And how long has it been? It seems like just yesterday."

"Oh… I think maybe two years, maybe three years, ma'am," Lopez replied. "I had my photo taken with you when you were attending a meeting at Quantico."

"I remember." And now Fay did remember. "But it seems someone received a promotion since then," she commented.

"Yes, ma'am." As the two continued to walk, Lopez said, "The photo meant a lot to me. I sent it to my parents. But, ma'am, I lost the photo."

Fay stopped walking. She had noticed an American flag, one which she thought it to be a one hundred-year-old version, or older, mounted on the wall nearby the elevator. "Why don't you and I walk back to the flag down there?" she suggested, pointing in the direction of the flag. "We will get a selfie. You have your cell, don't you?"

"Yes, ma'am."

When the two reached the flag near the elevator, the door was opening. A man emerged. Fay asked, "Sir, could I bother you for a moment. Quick picture?" She gestured to the man the photo would be of her and Lopez.

"Sure," the man replied.

Lopez handed the man her cell. In so doing, Fay noticed an odd look on Lopez's face, as if she was now unsure of this picture-taking business.

The two women posed for three photos. Before handing the cell back to Fay, the man asked, "May I have a photo as well?"

Fay was clueless as to who the guy was, or why he had asked for a photo. "Of what, or who?" she asked him.

Lopez jumped in to save the day. "We would be happy to, Ambassador Levine."

Of course, Fay thought, *U.S. Ambassador to Egypt Levine*. "So nice to meet you, Mr. Ambassador," Fay said and extended her hand.

The Ambassador shook her hand. "Commander Green," he replied, "I must admit since your time in the White House, I have been somewhat of a fan."

"You are too kind, sir."

"What brings you here, Commander Green?" the Ambassador asked Fay.

Fay gave him a quick synopsis of her impending dilemma, while the Ambassador listened with sympathy.

"You are meeting with Adel then," the Ambassador said once Fay had finished. "Her office is on the way to mine. I will walk with you. Have you met Adel before?"

"No, sir," Fay replied.

"I will introduce the two of you."

The Ambassador's plush office was the first along the hallway. The three paused there for several professional quality photos, which would find their way into a frame and then onto an office wall.

Although the photo diversion had somewhat hindered Fay from her urgent meeting with Officer

McKinny, Corporal Lopez's inadvertent photo op actually proved beneficial. Fay now had the Ambassador's attention and potential involvement in helping her find Katrinka.

The trio arrived at Adel McKinny's office. Ambassador Levine opened the door to McKinny's outer office, allowing the two women to precede him in. An aide rose from behind his desk to greet the Ambassador and his party.

Ambassador Levine made the introductions. "David, Commander Green and Corporal Lopez, her aide, here to see Adel."

Aide? I have an aide? Fay thought. *Sweet!*

"Welcome, all. Mrs. McKinny is expecting you," David said. "I will inform her you are here." David pointed to the furnishings in McKinny's outer office.

No sooner had they sat than McKinny entered from her inner office. There was a broad smile on her face. "Commander Green," she said, "I have been looking forward to meeting with you. I am sorry the purpose of your visit is unpleasant. But do come in!"

After they had entered McKinny's office, she said, "Please, make yourselves comfortable."

As soon as all were sitting, McKinny asked, "Refreshments, anyone? How about you, Corporal Lopez?"

Lopez was shy. And rightly so. She had, within a matter of minutes, transitioned from one world into another. "Can I have a cola, ma'am?" she requested. Her voice had a hint of hopefulness in it.

McKinny smiled, "And for you Commander Green?"

"Cola for me, as well. Please," Fay said.

McKinny turned to Ambassador Levine. "The usual tea, Ambassador?" she guessed.

"Yes, please."

McKinny stood. "I will be right back."

Within a few minutes, McKinny returned with a tray and the refreshments. She offered each their beverage of choice. Then she returned to her chair behind the massive cherry desk. "Commander Green. How can we help?" she started.

Fay downloaded her story, covering how and why she, Katrinka, and her family had arrived in Cairo. She thought it wise to be as transparent with the Embassy staff as possible. "Lady Katrinka is an heir apparent to the Duchy of Russia," Fay explained. "I and her guardians, Russian Navy Captain Alexander Lavrov and Russian Navy Commander Irena Sergeevna, have escorted Lady Katrinka to Cairo for a one-week visit. We are staying at Sofitel Cairo Nile El Gezirah." She continued to explain Katrinka and Irishka had planned to meet in the hotel lobby for a swim date. According to a man at reception, he had noticed Kat talking to two men who he had assumed to be Egyptian police. Fay had found Kat's cell on a chair in the hotel lobby. She went on to explain Captain Lavrov and Commander Sergeevna were meeting with someone at the Russian Embassy.

Mrs. McKinny was taking notes fast and furiously. Ambassador Levine displayed a frown and maintained a stoic expression as he listened to Fay.

Levine spoke. "Mrs. McKinny, this is your meeting. I have intruded. Do you mind if I interject?"

"Please, sir," McKinny said, "Mi casa es su casa."

"Thank you, Adel." The Ambassador turned to

address Fay. "The Department of State is committed to ensuring fair and humane treatment for U.S. citizens imprisoned overseas," he said. "We stand ready to assist incarcerated citizens and their families within the limits of our authority in accordance with international, domestic and foreign law. Where this gets sticky is Lady Katrinka is not a U.S. citizen. Am I correct?"

"Mr. Ambassador, Adel, Katrinka is my adopted daughter," Fay told them. "We are in the process of applying for naturalization. She now holds a Russian passport."

"Because she is adopted by a U.S. citizen and because she is adopted by a serving member of the U.S. Armed Forces, we may be able to work with it," the Ambassador decided. "Do you concur, Adel?"

"I agree," McKinny said, "I will have legal look into it. But we need to get on this ASAP. So, with your permission Mr. Levine, my recommendation is we proceed until notified otherwise."

Ambassador Levine added, "Commander Green, my office will contact the local authorities on your behalf."

"Thank you both. This is more than I had hoped for," Fay said. "My years of experience when dealing with our personnel detained in jails around the world has taught me the initial confusion and disorientation is difficult. Katrinka does not speak Arabic, know the customs, nor the Egyptian legal system."

"We, from time to time, receive requests from Americans who have been arrested in Egypt," Levine said. "I am sorry to say the Egyptian police are not always cooperative. Fortunately, we have built several strong relationships with local police officials. I will make a few inquiries. I promise we will get a few answers for you in quick order. You should retain an English-speaking lawyer," the Ambassador went on. "I have a referral for you. When we locate her, you will be able to visit with her. Bring reading material and vitamins with you. We will help you establish a bank account. You may need funds for both the lawyer and for the court or police, I am sorry to say."

"What would you suggest in the way of funds?" Fay asked.

Mrs. McKinny said, "For a third world nation, U.S. currency has strength. I recommend perhaps ten thousand U.S."

"Not a problem, Adel."

"You well know, Commander Green," Levine said, "the Embassy cannot be involved in any way regarding court involvement. I can advise the lawyer we will refer you to is one of the best at his skill. Other than an English-speaking lawyer, do you have someone who has been acting as an Arabic guide while you are visiting Cairo?"

"No," Fay replied. "I had not thought about it, to be honest."

The Ambassador's eyes traveled to Corporal Lopez. "Adel, will you have David contact First Sergeant Grace?" he requested. "If he can meet us here, we would appreciate it."

Mrs. McKinny called her aide, David, on the office intercom. "David, if you can locate First Sergeant Grace for us, ask him to meet with us ASAP," she instructed. "Thank you, David."

Ambassador Levine asked, "Corporal Lopez, I understand you are one of our Arabic speakers?"

Corporal Lopez replied, "I can speak it but am weak on reading and writing, sir."

"Speaking is sufficient," the Ambassador reassured her. "I am going to ask First Sergeant Grace if he will agree to the Embassy request for your TDA transfer to the U.S. Navy and Commander Green as her aide while she resides in Cairo. Is it okay with you?"

Lopez had a hard time not showing her enthusiasm. She was a Marine through and through. "Yes, sir," she replied.

David announced, "Marine First Sergeant Grace is here, ma'am."

"Please ask him to come in, David."

There came a knock at the door. "Come in, Mr. Grace," McKinny said.

Grace opened the door and immediately noticed Fay. Per protocol, he saluted her. "Ma'am," he said.

Fay replied, "Please join us, First Sergeant."

McKinny offered, "Please, First Sergeant, have a seat. Can I offer you a refreshment?"

Grace considered her offer. "Sparkling water," he replied.

"Why not begin our request to the First Sergeant while I get the water?" McKinny suggested to the others before leaving the room.

"Commander Green has a temporary duty assignment request of you, Mr. Grace," Ambassador Levine informed him.

Sergeant Grace nodded.

McKinny returned with Sergeant Grace's sparkling water.

Fay began, "It is good to meet you, Sergeant Grace."

"Likewise, ma'am."

"Mr. Grace, I find myself in need of an aide while conducting my business here in Cairo," Fay said. "My request is an unusual one. Would Corporal Lopez be available to me, and would she be allowed one to two weeks leave of absence while she assists me?" Fay could not ask the Marine Corps to provide to her an assistant at taxpayer expense.

"Providing Corporal Lopez is willing to request a fourteen day leave of absence, I will authorize it," Grace agreed. "What she does in her free time is her choice."

Lopez said, "Sir, I would like to formally request an emergency fourteen-day leave. Effective today." She added, "Thank you, sir."

Grace smiled. "This is a difficult choice for me," he said. "You are asking me to give up one of my best for two weeks. But, yes, I will process the paperwork, if you wish to spend your leave with Commander Green."

Corporal Lopez, with her face still full of excitement, asked, "May I be dismissed, First Sergeant?"

First Sergeant Grace replied, "You are dismissed, Corporal."

Lopez rose from her seat. As she proceeded toward the door, Fay called after her, "Hold up there, Lopez."

Lopez came to a halt. "Ma'am?"

"Pack your civvies but I want you to wear your uniform when you leave the Embassy with me," Fay instructed her. "Meet me back here or in the Ambassador's office."

"Yes, ma'am." Lopez again started toward the door.

"And, Lopez, don't forget to stop by my office," Grace told her. "I need your signature on the leave papers."

After Lopez had shut the door behind her, Grace turned back to the group. "Youthful enthusiasm," he commented, "I could use a hundred more like her."

Fay thanked Mrs. McKinny and the Ambassador for their kind help. Ambassador Levine invited Fay to wait for Corporal Lopez in his office.

Thirty minutes had passed before Lopez arrived fresh and ready for her new assignment.

The Embassy called a cab for the women. Lopez and Fay proceeded to the Embassy gate.

As they approached the gate, the Marine guard snapped to attention and saluted Fay and Lopez. A guard opened the gate and the two women passed through. Fay noticed Lopez could not help but give her friends a tiny wave. Otherwise, they would have been left to wonder if their friend were perhaps in big trouble and on her way to the brig.

After Lopez's gear was secure in the trunk and with the women safely buckled in, the cab sped off. Fay gave the driver the hotel address and settled in for the ride.

Along the way, Fay wanted to know more about her new protégée. "Lopez, please tell me you do have a first name," she said.

"Thank you, ma'am. My name is Azrael, but friends and family call me Jimmi," the other woman responded.

"If I recall my Bible, Azrael is one of God's angels," Fay said.

"Yes, ma'am. An archangel. Azrael is God's

angel," Lopez said. "I think you know, ma'am, Azrael in some cultures is Lucifer and Amenadiel's sister and the Angel of Death."

"I do recall it," Fay remarked

"When I was a child, for obvious reasons I did not like the name, so I went by Jimmi for years," Lopez explained. "When I joined the Marines, the name Azrael came back. But something different happened. My Marine friends would always tell my name was badass. With me being a Marine, it seemed to fit. So here I am, Azrael."

"For what it is worth, Azrael," Fay told her, "I like it! But what do you want me to call you?"

"Azrael, or Az. Either way," Azrael replied.

"Going forward, we are off duty," Fay said. "We are going to put aside the 'ma'am' and 'sir.' Habit is habit but give it a try. I am Fay. We are going to meet two more of my crew at the hotel. Sasha is a Captain and a lawyer in the Russian Navy. Irishka is a Commander and a commando in the Russian Navy as well."

"A real Russian commando…wow!" Azrael exclaimed. "Is she a badass, Fay?"

Fay chuckled. "That she is, but she is also a very nice woman. You will like her."

Azrael seemed hesitant to ask, but did anyway. "Ma'am, Fay… may I ask, are we going to save a real princess?"

"Well, she is not yet a princess. We could call her a lady in waiting, if you like," Fay replied.

"Wow," Azrael said. "I grew up in East L.A., Fay. There is nothing there for a Latino girl like me. I had to get out. The Marine Corps saved me."

"Your family must be proud," Fay stated. "You are a Marine Embassy Guard."

"My parents are most proud, Fay. My dad always brags about me to his friends."

Fay asked, "Will you retire from the Marines?"

'It is my plan," Azrael replied. "I hope not to retire as an MSG, however."

"Oh?" Fay asked. "What is your dream?"

"It is an impossible dream for an East L.A. kid like me," Azrael said.

"I learned a long time ago, nothing is impossible. Hang on to the dream," Fay encouraged her. "Perhaps when we get our princess back, you and I can sit for a session of career planning. Okay?"

"I would appreciate the help, ma'am."

It was early evening when the two women arrived at the hotel. Fay had texted Sasha asking he and Irishka meet her and their new aide in the hotel's lobby.

Fay quickly found Irishka and Sasha in the lobby. After introducing Azrael, Fay was anxious to learn what news Sasha and Irishka had uncovered at the Russian Embassy. And she was equally anxious to tell them about her meeting at the U.S. Embassy.

With the exception of Azrael, no one else had eaten since prior to Katrinka's disappearance. It was now a waiting game until word came from the Embassy. During dinner, Sasha shared his news from the Russian Embassy, which was similar to Fay's. The Russian Ambassador thought because Russia had a better relationship with Egypt than the U.S., it would be advisable for Sasha and Irishka to work through the Russian Embassy. They all agreed to use the services of the English-speaking lawyer recommended to Fay by the U.S. Embassy. It was thought Azrael's proficiency in the Arabic language and her knowledge of the city would be of immense help in their quest to find and free Katrinka.

Chapter 3

Earlier, Fay had called the lawyer recommended to her by the U.S. Embassy. Hassan Hafeez, Attorney at Law, had suggested he meet with Fay at 8:30 A.M. at her hotel. Fay was able to reserve one of the hotel's conference rooms for the meeting.

Hassan was prompt. Fay met him in the hotel lobby and walked with him to the conference room where Sasha, Azrael, and Irishka were waiting. When all had settled in the room, Fay introduced Hassan to her group. Coffee and tea service was provided by hotel staff shortly after.

Fay began, "Mr. Hafeez, thank you so much for agreeing to meet with us. I was not able to tell you much on the phone about our problem. You come highly recommended by the U.S. Embassy."

"Thank you, Miss Green," Hafeez returned her greeting. "I am confident I may be of assistance to you. My firm has experience in representing those from foreign countries who travel to Egypt."

"We are thankful, Mr. Hafeez. I said to you on the phone both Mr. Lavrov and I are lawyers and yet we feel we may be like fish out of water, so to speak, when it comes to Egyptian law," Fay told him.

"You will be surprised, Miss Green. I know something of your law," Hafeez replied. "You will find ours is not much different from yours. Our challenge is one of politics, and not law."

Hafeez removed a note pad and pen from his briefcase. He also removed a small recording device. "Is it allowable for me to record a portion of our conversation for my later reference?" he requested.

Sasha and Fay agreed.

Fay proceeded to outline the events leading up to Katrinka's disappearance. Hafeez made diligent notes and asked often for clarification on a few of the points. When Fay had finished, Hafeez asked if he could review with them to ensure he understood the events leading up to Katrinka's disappearance.

Hafeez reviewed his notes. "You said both the Russian Embassy and the U.S. Embassy have a photocopy of Miss - or is it Lady Lavrova's passport?"

"Yes," Sasha replied. "For now, we refer to her as Miss Lavrova."

"How is her name on the passport?" Hafeez asked next.

"Yekaterina Lavrova," Sasha said.

Irishka's body language suggested she had something to add.

"Irishka, what do you have to say?" Fay asked her.

"Katrinka was known by 'Markova' while serving in Navy," she said.

Hafeez noted it. "So, if she were detained by Egyptian Police, she would be known by either Lavrova or Markova?"

"Yes," Fay replied. "But her passport indicates Lavrova." Fay asked, "What are you thinking, Hassan?"

"I want to interview the hotel staff who were on duty in the lobby area at the time Miss Lavrova was detained," Hafeez stated. "It is unusual for uniformed police to so quickly detain anyone. It sounds like she was here one minute and disappeared the next."

"Do you suppose Katrinka was apprehended by someone other than local police?" Fay asked the lawyer.

"These men may not be local police but instead Egyptian intelligence officers," Hafeez speculated. "Unfortunately, our system is quick by your standards. Miss Lavrova may be detained for as briefly as twelve hours before being referred to a trial. There has been a movement of late where security forces are detaining journalists, lawyers, and human rights activists on charges of terrorism."

"Twelve hours has long past, Hassan," Fay reminded him. "Is it possible Katrinka has been referred to trial?"

"Article 54 of our constitution allows that personal freedom is a natural right and cannot be infringed upon. Except in cases of *in flagrante delicto*," Hafeez added, "which would not have been possible."

"What does the article allow for search and seizure, Hassan?" Sasha asked.

"Citizens may only be searched, arrested and apprehended, Mr. Lavrov."

"What of their freedoms restricted by a warrant?" Sasha followed up.

"Those whose freedoms have been restricted are supposed to be informed of the reason for their apprehension," Hafeez explained. "They are notified of their rights. When they arrive at a jail or prison, they are notified of their rights in writing. In Miss Lavrova's case, she would not be able to read it, unless she can read Arabic."

Lavrov said, "Arabic is one of the languages she does not read."

"I have several worries," Hafeez told the group. "However, the constitution also allows that when an arrest is made, the detainee be allowed to immediately contact their family and lawyer and be brought before the investigating authority within twenty-four hours of their freedoms having been restricted."

"It is possible then because Katrinka is Russian citizen and not Egyptian," Sasha asked, "the arresting authority is not affording her any of the Article 54 rights?"

"Not likely," Hafeez concluded. "But anything is possible these days. My guess, she is being detained until Egyptian intelligence can determine what her charge might be."

"If she were not arrested by local police and it was Egyptian intelligence, where would they hold her?" Fay asked.

"My guess is Egypt's State Information Service would hold her at Tora prison in Cairo."

Fay said, "We must go there."

"It is not so easy as visit to jail in the United States," Hafeez warned. "Permission or other documents may be required. I think you could try to obtain such from the Russian Embassy."

Lavrov said he would call the Embassy immediately.

In the meantime, Hafeez recommended an attempt should be made to verify if Katrinka was being held at Tora. "I will go there immediately." He turned his attention to Azrael. "I recommend Miss Lopez accompany me, in her uniform." Hassan went on to explain, "Lawyers are not in favor with the political system. Women are not in favor either. They do respect a uniform, however. I believe because Miss Lopez is an Arabic speaker and because she does wear the uniform of an Embassy guard, we may get beyond the first door."

Fay turned to Azrael. "Are you up for this?" she asked.

"Fay, I am a United States Marine. I am up for anything and everything," Azrael assured her.

Fay conveyed a warm smile to Azrael.

"This will be good.," Hassan said. "We will leave immediately. Do you have niqab, Miss Lopez?"

"Yes, in my room."

"I believe the uniform, your dark hair and skin, and the niqab will be an impressive and official distraction for us," Hafeez stated.

Fay more than appreciated Hassan's fast response. "Sasha and I will call the embassies with an update," she said. "Shall we go with you?"

"I think not. Americans are not in favor near this prison," Hafeez answered. "My feeling is because Miss Lavrova is Russian, to have more Russian show up may not be a good idea either. I also believe Egyptian security forces must know who Miss Lavrova is, or they suspect she is someone they wish to detain." Hafeez paused as if to plan his next response. "If…and understand I can only assume…because Miss Lavrova is Russian, and should her background reveal a military history, police will suspect espionage agent connections. Now we would have problem we did not have before. Spies are executed without delay here in Egypt."

****

Katrinka was shown to a chair placed across from Azrael. To Azrael, Katrinka's demeanor was both wary and guarded. Lopez removed her niqab and smiled. She retrieved a note pad and pen from a pouch she had been allowed to enter the room with. Speaking loudly enough for the three guards in the room to hear, she said, "Miss Lavrova, I am Azrael Lopez from the U.S. Embassy Security Guard." As she spoke, she discreetly pushed a scrap of paper toward Katrinka.

Katrinka palmed the paper in her right hand but continued to remain silent. Lopez had been briefed by Fay to use the word "sweetie" when she first addressed Katrinka.

"I am here to help, Sweetie," Azrael said.

Katrinka, who had yet to speak, covertly glanced at the scrap of paper. It read: *Trust her - Faya*. Katrinka acknowledged with a nod.

"Miss Lavrova," Azrael asked her, "have you been charged?"

Katrinka shook her head, no.

"Have you been treated well?"

Katrinka nodded, yes.

"Have you been advised of your rights?" Azrael followed up.

A slow shake of the head, to indicate "no," was Katrinka's only response.

"We have retained a lawyer. If you will meet with Mr. Hassan Hafeez, he represents you," Azrael informed her.

Katrinka pointed toward Azrael's pen.

She discreetly pushed the pen across the table to Katrinka. Katrinka slipped the pen up her right sleeve.

"I am going to report back to the U.S. Embassy that you are well and not in need of medical attention," Azrael said next.

Katrinka glanced in the direction of the guards. They were distracted by a fourth man who had entered the room. She slipped the pen from her sleeve and quickly wrote something on the scrap of paper. She then slipped the pen up her sleeve and pushed the scrap of paper back to Azrael, who palmed the paper.

"Miss Lavrova, I will consult with my superiors and my hope is either Mr. Hafeez or myself will be back to you soon." Azrael conveyed a look of hope as she said, "Hang in there. We have your six." She smiled again as she rose from the chair.

Azrael returned to Hassan, who had waited for her in the lobby. "Let's go," she said.

During the ride back to the hotel, Azrael relayed verbatim the one-way conversation she had had with Katrinka. At some point in the transit from prison to hotel, Azrael became drowsy and fell asleep.

Fay, Sasha, and Irishka were anxiously waiting for them in the lobby. Fay recommended they adjourn to her room.

At the hotel, Hassan began, "Azrael did a great job. Thanks to her, we now have a sense of direction. The good news is Miss Katrinka is medically fit. She has indicated she has not been charged nor has she been advised of her rights. Basically, they are holding her…without reason."

"This is the first time in my life I communicated with someone and they did not say a word," Azrael commented. "I sense Lady Katrinka is a lovely woman."

Fay smiled and asked Hassan, "Is it allowable or in keeping with Egyptian law?"

"No. But there is little we can do," he replied.

"I have a note from Katrinka for you, ma'am," Azrael said to Fay, handing her the note.

Fay reviewed the note. It was written in Russian. Fay passed the note to Sasha, who then passed it on to Irishka.

Irishka's expression changed to one of concern. "Katrinka has written, 'Khoroshko is dead.'" She said to Sasha, "*Sluzhba bezpeky Ukrayiny.*"

Sasha told the others, "An agent with Security Service of Ukraine is dead. It would not be unreasonable to assume Katrinka has been involved. She most likely has been implicated in murder of the Ukraine agent."

"Why? How?" Fay asked.

"Sasha says Khoroshko is an agent with Ukraine spy agency," Irishka explained. "He is dangerous man. In past, he has attempted to kill me. I thought SSU had forgotten about me. Apparently not."

"You have a theory, Irishka?" Sasha asked.

"Khoroshko followed me to Cairo with intent to eliminate me," Irishka speculated. "Katrinka knows this man. She may have spotted him near hotel. To protect me, she may well have killed him. I would do same for her."

Azrael had been intently listening. In fact, Fay worried Azrael was way beyond her pay grade by now. Embassy guards were not of the espionage kind.

Azrael surprised Fay when she offered, "In a time of war, we all willingly put our lives on the line for our fellow soldiers and for our countries."

In light, Fay reasoned, rather than being a random killer, Katrinka was performing her military duty and protecting the life of a comrade.

Chapter 4

Three long and frustrating days passed. The Embassies were, for the time being, powerless. Hassan had made two trips to the prison seeking guidance from the authorities. He was given a stack of documents to process, which he turned his attention to immediately.

On the afternoon of the third day, Azrael and Hassan traveled to the prison. Fay had sent several bottles of water and vitamins along with Azrael. Azrael texted Fay to inform her they had arrived at the prison. Thirty minutes later, Fay's cell chimed. She knew the call was from Azrael.

Her excitement was evident in her voice. "Ma'am, Lady Katrinka is not here!" Azrael exclaimed.

Horror filled Fay's heart. "Azrael, start at the beginning. Take a breath."

"We arrived. They had us wait for like half an hour," Azrael recounted. "Then a man came to us. He said Lady Katrinka was not there. We asked him where she was. He would not tell us."

"What! How could they not know?" Fay gasped.

Hassan came on the phone. "Hello Fay, she is not here. But I wondered about it. The man we spoke to did not say but I know man at prison. He told me she escaped."

Fay had one more "what" left in her. "WHAT?!" she cried.

Irishka and Sasha were with Fay but had not heard the conversation. "I am going to put you on speaker, Hassan," Fay said to him. "Tell us again."

"I was told by friend at the prison Miss Katrinka escaped early this morning," Hafeez repeated.

"We are all in shock here, Hassan. Do you have other details?" Fay asked.

"Unfortunate, I only could learn this much." Hafeez apologized.

As Fay listened to Hassan, she noticed a smile had formed on Irishka's lips. "Hold on, Hassan." Fay turned her attention to Irishka. "What do you know, Irishka?" she asked.

"I know Katrinka is Russian, she is one of best operatives in Russia, she is clever, and she had pen given to her by Azrael. What else can I say?" Irishka replied.

Fay had not been aware Azrael had given Katrinka a pen. "You gave her a pen, Azrael, and they let her keep it?" she asked.

"Yes. She concealed it in her sleeve."

Irishka continued to smile. "This may not seem it, but it is good," she stated. Fay knew Irishka to be a pragmatic woman. Irishka said, "She escape, she lives. She stays, she dies. She knows it is truth."

Fay asked, "What are we to do, Irishka?

"We wait for her to contact us," Irishka advised. "When it is safe for her, she will tell us."

Hassan said, "We will be watched. The authorities will believe she will try to come to you. We should act as if we do not know of her escapade and remain concerned."

"Very well, business as usual," Fay said.

Hassan would return to his office with the intent of continuing the mound of paperwork that had been bestowed upon him by the Egyptian prison system.

Fay had several more questions. All bid Hassan farewell. Fay placed a room service order.

Irishka continued to add details in the form of theories. It was unusual for such a pragmatic woman to deal in theory, yet her assumptions were based on her own spy school training and what she knew of Katrinka's temperament and former training as well.

"Because Ukraine agents are known sometime to travel in pairs," Irishka said, "Katrinka's instincts are good so she will try to put distance between us. She will leave Egypt and head for a Russian friendly country. I think Cyprus."

"Will she contact us?" Fay asked.

"I do not think so. If she suspects second agent, she will want to lure him or her away. In other words, Kat will become mouse." Irishka concluded. "She knows I will know this so she will not try to let us know she is okay."

"It is dangerous," Fay stated.

"Very," Sasha said. "I believe she will contact us, but we cannot go to her until she asks for us. But not worry so much. For now, Irishka is correct, mouse is Kat."

"So, we wait," Fay confirmed.

It was probably wise for Sasha to change the subject when he did. "Have you yet visited pyramid and Sphinx, Faya?" Sasha asked.

"How can I?" Fay asked him.

"You can and you should. Azrael will be good guide for you," Sasha replied. "Katrinka will contact

Irishka. But we may wait for one week, I do not know."

Irishka offered reassurance. "Faya, while you wait, will you not eat? No, so while you wait, you must see. You must not let this consume you. It will. And then you are no good for anyone if your mind is not fresh for next step."

Azrael offered, "I have one week leave. I would like to show you the sights of Cairo."

Fay was hesitant but accepted. "Okay. Why don't we begin the tour tomorrow?"

****

08:15 hours, hotel, the following morning

Fay's night had been filled with a fitful sleep, although she did not feel tired when she met with Azrael for breakfast in the hotel coffee shop. Azrael recommended they hire a car for the thirty-mile drive to Saqqara to tour the world's oldest step pyramid.

Azrael said, "Ma'am, when we first met, you asked me about career choices and if I were to remain in the Marines, what I would like to do. I told you I had a dream that seemed impossible."

"And I told you anything was possible," Fay recapped.

"My dream was to fly. A helicopter pilot."

Fay said, with a note of encouragement in her voice, "I see it as a possible dream for you."

"Yes, but after working with Mr. Hafeez, you, and Mr. Lavrov…he is a lawyer, right?"

"Yes, he is a lawyer," Fay confirmed, "as I am, but in the Russian military system."

"I am thinking law," Azrael told her. "The talk of the constitution, working with Lady Lavrova's tragic case, our meeting at the Embassy. I don't know, it seems exciting to me."

"It seems exciting?"

"Yes, ma'am."

"I will admit at times it is," Fay said. "And at times it can be tedious as well."

"Ma'am, standing in the hot sun all day long can be tedious," Azrael replied. "Geez, at least I would be doing something of value. And maybe even in an air-conditioned office?"

Fay laughed. "You have impressed me in more ways than you know, Azrael." Fay paused while the waiter served their breakfasts. Then she said, "I have a staff of people who work with me, including my sister, who are known as Legalmen. You know of them?"

"Yes, ma'am, but I heard I would have to be super smart to do that kind of work," Azrael responded.

"Well, here is a news flash for you," Fay said. "You are 'super-smart,' you just don't know it."

"Thank you, Fay."

"If you are truly interested, I know people," Fay went on. "If you would do a bit of research, I will strike a bargain with you. When I get back, I will ask around. You tell me if it is the direction you want to take and I will help you to make it happen." Fay smiled. "How does that sound?"

Azrael shrieked. "Wow! Thank you, Fay!"

"No, thank you. For any career path to be meaningful and fun – yes, fun - enthusiasm and desire is essential," Fay told her.

Fay spotted Sasha entering the coffee shop. She waved to gain his attention.

Sasha's mood was happy when he approached the women's table. "Good morning, ladies," he greeted them.

Fay asked Sasha to join them. "Any news from the Russian Embassy?"

"None," Sasha replied. "I had small hope Katrinka went to embassy to seek asylum. I asked them to contact the Russian Embassy in Nicosia in the event Katrinka found her way to Cyprus. She may seek asylum there."

"Oh! Geez!" Azrael exclaimed. "There's been an explosion at the French Embassy." She was reading a text from her phone. "All embassies in Cairo have locked down. No one in, no one out." She continued to monitor her cell. "First Sergeant Grace is texting me." Azrael intently scanned her cell. "He asks me to stay away from the Embassy." She continued to scan her cell. "He says he will contact me when the Embassy reopens." Azrael looked up from her cell. "What do I do, ma'am? What about my friends?" she wondered.

Fay's cell chimed. She smiled. Fay read the text aloud, "First Sergeant says to tell you your leave has been suspended. You have been temporarily assigned to me."

"Ma'am?" Azrael questioned.

"First Sergeant did us a favor," Fay realized. "You are now TDY. I am sure First Sergeant has, or will, ensure that you will receive per-diem pay. Meals, lodging, and other expenses are covered for a few days. However, I will continue to cover those expenses for you. You are welcome to keep the guaranteed pay."

"I hope my friends will be okay," Azrael said.

"I am sure all will be fine, Azrael," Sasha said. "In the meantime, you can continue to help us."

Azrael smiled. "Have I been a help to you, sir?"

Sasha replied, "Very much so."

****

4:30 P.M., Limassol New Port, Cyprus

The tourist dressed in white shorts and running shoes, a tangerine top, a ball cap, sunglasses, and a red backpack descended the gang plank from the ship to the dock at Cruise Ships Dock at Limassol, New Port. Once on the dock, she paused to ensure the two men lurking in the shadows of the terminal building had noticed her. She hailed a cab. Her destination was the Russian Embassy in the nearby capitol of Nicosia.

The trip to the embassy would take almost two hours. Occasionally, she checked to be sure the men were keeping up with her. She wanted to know where they were at all times. Each morning, she began her day with but one simple rule Irishka has once taught her: "Every morning in Africa, a gazelle wakes up. It knows it must run faster than the fastest lion or it will be killed. Every morning, a lion wakes up. It knows it must outrun the slowest gazelle or it will starve to death. It doesn't matter whether you're a lion or gazelle. When the sun comes up, you'd better be running." *I must run today. Every day. Without fail*, Kat thought.

The past week had been somewhat stressful. When she had been arrested in Cairo, Egyptian security forces had seemed to think she had assassinated a Ukrainian agent, a chap who had had designs on assassinating her Irishka. Yet, she had been able to turn the tables. Her stint in prison had lasted three days, with the aid of a U.S. Marine and U.S. Embassy guard. Now, that in itself would be a story she could tell the grandkids one day. With no ID, money, and dressed in the uniform given to her at the prison, she had made her way to the

Israeli port city of Ashdod. There, she had boarded a cruise ship bound for Cyprus. Her travel from Cairo to Ashdod had been slow because the Ukrainian agents who were trailing her were having a hard time keeping up.

She had made a mistake when she had lost them in Ashdod. They knew which ship she had boarded. They would have to catch up with her in Cyprus. Her immediate plan was to seek refuge in the Russian Embassy, then head on to Paris to find a friend who would help her refresh and regroup. At some point, when she felt she had the Ukrainians' full and undivided attention, she would deal with them.

Chapter 5

The cab left her at the Russian Embassy gate. She was now faced with a challenge: how to gain access to the embassy without the cost of admission or an ID. Her quest began with a conversation with one of the embassy guards, a nice boy from Astrakhan. It did not seem lost on the boy that a *"khoroshen'kaya zhenshchina"* ("pretty woman") had decided to afford him the time of day. Perhaps it was her hazel eyes, the shoulder length auburn hair, or her long legs? At some point, the young man had decided he had asked enough questions and she was allowed in. Her backpack was searched, as was she, which in her mind took a little longer than the standard pat down would normally take. There seemed to be a lot of patting, anyway.

One of the guards escorted her to the lobby area. She was introduced to the receptionist, who in turn asked her to be seated. Perhaps thirty minutes had passed when she spotted a man, who was smiling, descending the white marble staircase. His eyes were glued on her.

When he drew near, he extended his right hand toward her and said, "Lady Yekaterina!" Their conversation continued in Russian. "How nice of you to visit us! Welcome. I am Ambassador Aleksey Breznov here in Cyprus. How can I be of service?"

Katrinka firmly shook the Ambassador's hand. His

introduction told her he had spent time vetting her. He knew she was at least former Navy intelligence. Katrinka was surprised he knew of her ancestry. She, herself, had only recently found out.

"Please, come to my office." He extended his hand toward her again. "Please allow me to carry your luggage," Breznov said.

Katrinka handed her backpack to Mr. Breznov and the two proceeded to his second-floor office. It was now 7:30 P.M.

Breznov's office was fitting for an ambassador, with a high ceiling, a large desk, and plush chairs. He offered Katrinka a seat. "Lady Lavrova, I understand you have had a long journey to reach us," he began.

"I have been traveling seven days since Cairo," Katrinka confirmed.

Breznov had her sense of humor apparently. He asked, "Seven days? And the camel?"

Katrinka smiled. "Yes. He died from too much walking," she retorted.

Breznov laughed. "It is getting late. I would like to offer you food and drink. Please, we will go to dining room." He stood and motioned for her to follow him.

Katrinka had not had anything in the way of decent food or drink since she had left Cairo almost a week earlier. This could prove to be a great thing!

A woman entered the room. Katrinka assumed her to be Mrs. Breznov.

It was. The Ambassador stood to make the introduction. "Lady Lavrova, may I introduce you to my wife, Annastasia Breznova Chase."

Annastasia extended her hand and smiled as she approached Katrinka. "Lady Lavrova," she said in greeting. "Welcome. It is an honor to meet one from our royal family. Please, sit."

Katrinka sat again. "Mrs. Breznova," she returned, "thank you for your hospitality."

"Please, please, my Lady, you must call us Annastasia and Alexey," Annastasia insisted.

"You have had a long journey," Alexey said. "You must be famished. Shall we dine?"

Katrinka nodded. She could not recall when she had last had anything more substantial than a soda cracker or something she had snatched from a plate at an outdoor café.

An embassy staff person had been waiting for the evening dinner order. Alexey summoned him. "Oleg, what are we serving this evening?"

"For this evening, sir, we are serving local sea bass and potatoes. And, of course, soup."

"Excellent! The service will be for three this evening," Alexey said. "Please begin with coffee and best wine. Your recommendation, Oleg."

"Thank you, sir." Oleg left the table.

The dinner proved as filling as it was delightful. Following an exhilarating conversation, Katrinka begged to retire. Alexey and Annastasia bid her good night. Katrinka had informed them she would depart in the morning. But first, she was made to promise she would stay for breakfast. It made sense to her. The journey ahead would be a long and arduous one.

****

9:30 P.M., Sofitel Bar Lounge, Cairo, Egypt

Azrael and Fay sat in the lounge, talking and watching the Nile flow past their table. "Worry" was the word of the week, yet Azrael was proving adept at keeping Fay's mind from excessive worry.

Fay's cell chimed. It was Sasha calling. She answered the call and put the phone on speaker. "Hi, Sasha," she said. "We are here in the Bar Lounge blowing bubbles and watching the Nile flow by. Where are you?"

"I am in my room. How is the Shisha?"

"Great! Come on down! You can party with us."

"Give me ten minutes," Sasha replied. "I have news."

Fay's excitement grew. "Is it Katrinka!?" she asked hopefully.

"Small news. I will explain when I get there."

Ten minutes was an eternity. Azrael and Fay ordered another round, including one for Sasha. Fay warned Azrael that Sasha, like all good Russians, enjoyed his vodka and she should not be tempted to drink very much of it. This was a lesson Fay had well learned the last time she had drank with Sasha a year or so ago.

Sasha arrived. To Fay, he did not seem to be concerned. She assumed his news was not disastrous. Sasha sat.

"What do we know, Sasha?" Fay asked.

"I received a call from the Russian Embassy about forty-five minutes ago," he began. "I know you would want to know immediately, but I wanted to get completed information first."

"She is okay, Sasha?" Fay asked eagerly. Sasha could not divulge his information fast enough for her.

"She is now at Russian Embassy in Cyprus," Sasha said. "Irishka is preparing to leave for Cyprus as soon as we can get Katrinka's passport and credit cards from your room."

"Should we go now?" Fay wondered.

"Yes, I will deliver the documents to Irishka. She has 1:00 A.M. flight to Cyprus. She will deliver them to Katrinka in the morning."

Fay asked, "What are we to do?"

"As hard as it is, we are to remain here," Sasha told her. "Irishka will call me from Cyprus when she has more details."

"Hard to do, but okay," Fay agreed. "Let's get the documents from my room."

****

8:35 A.M., Russian Embassy, Nicosia, Cyprus

Katrinka was preparing for breakfast. She would depart shortly after. Her plan was to leave the island, make her way to a mainland port, and then go on to Paris. A knock came at the door.

"Embassy staff," the voice announced from the other side of the door.

Katrinka opened the door. An Embassy staff member handed her an envelope.

"Lady Lavrova," the staff person said, "this arrived for you by courier this morning."

Katrinka knew the courier could only have been Irishka. She thanked the staff person, closed the door, and went to a nearby table to open the envelope. It was as she had expected: her passport, credit card, debit card, and tickets. There was a cryptic note placed inside the passport. She knew it to be code. Irishka had written the address of a Russian safehouse in Paris. She reviewed the tickets, one for a ship departing tomorrow morning with a rail connection to Paris.

Katrinka placed everything in the pack and set off

to find Annastasia for their breakfast date. During the meal, Annastasia asked what time Katrinka planned to depart.

Katrinka said, "Thank you for asking. As a matter of fact, I received tickets just a few minutes ago. The ship I am to take leaves tomorrow morning. May I remain here until three A.M.?"

Annastasia was delighted. Perhaps it was because she had little contact with other Russian women on the island. The two women had an enjoyable breakfast. Annastasia asked, "Will you come with me outside?" She led Katrinka to a balcony overlooking a rear courtyard. "I hope you think me as friend?"

"Yes," Katrinka responded, "of course."

"Please, call me Nastasya," Annastasia requested. "I have concern for you, Katrinka. Today, you receive package from courier. Because of recent explosion at French Embassy, security in Near and Middle East is stricter. For security, all packages are scanned. They scan your package. Not unusual. But tickets from Cyprus to France."

Katrinka said, "I see how it looks. I come from city where French Embassy has bomb. I go to country of embassy. I arrive without papers and only clothes on my back."

"Yes," Annastasia replied. "Yet, you are Russian intelligence, and you are heir to Russian royal family. It is confirmed but it is confusing."

"I agree."

"I am practical woman, Lady Katrinka. Politics and terrorism are not for me," Annastasia stated. "My intuition tells me you are one to be trusted."

"I appreciate it, Nastasya. What do you think?"

Katrinka asked the other woman.

"You will be safe here. No one can touch you," Annastasia promised. "When you leave tomorrow, suspicion will follow. I think move quickly in dark and do not linger. If you have trouble before you leave Cyprus, you contact me. I will help."

"I appreciate your confidence."

"Now," Annastasia continued, "there is party tonight at Embassy. Some affluent people from city. It may be good for you to attend as friend of Russian Embassy. Russian Embassy would not harbor a terrorist."

Katrinka smiled and considered her blue jean and sweatshirt attire. "I own only these and shorts. Not for party, is it?"

"It is informal. Dinner, drinks, and some music," Annastasia assured her. "I will arrange for appropriate clothes. You like dress, or no?"

"I think, no," Katrinka decided.

****

Katrinka left the embassy at 5:00 A.M. The Akgunler Denizcilik ferry to Tasucu, Turkey from Kyrenia departed at 7:00 A.M. The travel time from Kyrenia was six hours. She did not see the Ukrainians and there were no cars following her from the embassy to Kyrenia.

She stood at the rail as the boat slipped away from the pier. The sun was rising over the crystal-clear Mediterranean. Annastasia had packed an apple, a banana, grapes, and a bottle of spring water for her. Katrinka hoped one day to return to Cyprus to visit with her new friend, Nastasya.

It was 1:30 P.M. when the boat arrived at Tasucu.

She waited again, looking for the Ukrainian agents. She did not see them. She decided for whatever reason these Ukrainian boys did not seem too adept at this agent business. She would travel by bus and train from Tasucu to Istanbul, then to Budapest and then Zurich, before finally making a four-hour trip on the TGV Lyria high-speed train to Paris's Gare de Lyon station. All in all, it was a three-and-a-half-day trip.

The two-hour bus to Karaman left the Tasucu station on time. The train and bus schedules were as dependable as time pieces. Train companies were anal about time schedules; on time, all of the time. An uneventful hour passed. Long distance travel by bus or train was boring. Anything nonproductive was boring, by Katrinka's standards. Scenery watching could be interesting at times, or people watching on occasion, as well. Her life often depended on astute people watching.

She thought about reading. Katrinka had nothing to read and the newspaper offerings were all in languages she did not understand, although a front-page photo on several of the daily newspapers being read by fellow passengers caught her eye. She asked the man sitting across from her if he spoke either English or Russian.

"Leetal of the English," he said.

She pointed to the photo displayed on the front page of the paper he was reading. "What is it?"

"French Embassy. Bomb."

"Where? When?" Katrinka asked.

"Cyprus. Early these morning?" he replied.

Chapter 6

8:30 A.M., Cairo, Egypt

Fay and Azrael sat in the hotel's Bar Lounge, enjoying the fresh, early Cairo morning, sipping on guava and mango juices. They had considered touring the Sphinx and the nearby pyramids at Giza or the Egyptian Museum. Anything to distract their thoughts from Katrinka. Fay's attention was focused on the Nile and the antics of a small aggressive duck who seemed to believe it owned the entire river, while Azrael's attention was focused on her cell.

"Ma'am, excuse me," Azrael broke in. "I don't want to interrupt your thoughts. I got a text from First Sergeant Grace."

"Oh? How is he?" Fay inquired.

"He says things are getting back to normal at the Embassy. He wanted me to know there was another bombing this morning at the French Embassy in Cyprus," Azrael said.

"I wonder what the French have done to offend someone?" wondered Fay.

"Bad batch of fries, ma'am," Azrael joked, before then saying, "Seriously, ma'am, I have been thinking about my friends and their safety since the first explosion."

"Now two." Fay reached for a banana. As she

peeled it, she asked, "How long has it been since you visited your home?"

"Seven months. I was going home next month," Azrael shared, "but this came up."

"Oh! Honey, I am sorry! Did I cause you not to go home?" Fay worried.

"Don't worry. I will get there. And to tell you the truth, I would not miss this for the world," Azrael admitted.

"For real?"

"Think how fate plays in our lives," Azrael told Fay. "You had come to the Embassy on a moment's notice because Lady Katrinka had been arrested. We had just had a shift change. Any one of the guards could have met you at the gate. But it was me. You did not have to ask me to escort you to the entry door. You asked me to accompany you to Mrs. McKinny's office. I asked for a selfie. Ambassador Levine was getting off the elevator. You asked him to take a photo. And we all ended up in Mrs. McKinny's office. Now, here I am. Sitting beside the Nile, drinking mango juice with a Navy Commander and lawyer, who was at one time the First Daughter. And I met a princess, in prison! How else can it happen? Fate, ma'am. Fate!"

"So, you are okay!?" Fay had to know.

Azrael reassured her, "Finer than a frog's hair, ma'am."

"A what's hair?" Fay asked, confused

"You know. A frog... ribbit ribbit?" Azrael imitated the animal. "My dad says it all of the time."

"Never heard that one before," Fay said, with a measure of doubt evident in her voice.

"Ma'am, can I ask something?" Azrael went on.

"You must have a ton of friends."

"Oh… not as many as you would think," Fay responded. "I consider myself to be a recluse. I like my privacy. Having to live in the White House for eight years was horrible for me."

"Do you think if Lady Katrinka decides to live in some rich place, she will feel the same way?"

"I hope not."

"Too much on our minds," Azrael said. "Do you feel like going to the Giza plateau and checking out the Sphinx and the pyramids?"

"Let's do it!" Fay exclaimed.

****

9:17 A.M., Karaman, Turkey

Katrinka hailed a cab for the three-mile ride to the Karaman station. She boarded the northbound train for the ninety-minute trip to Konya. During the transfer, she found an English language *Hürriyet Daily News* at a newsstand, along with a bottle of spring water. While she sipped on her water, she read the report of the French embassy bombing in Cyprus. Like the Cairo bombing, no one, or affiliated group, had claimed responsibility. Reading was a distraction. She had learned how to read while remaining observant at the same time.

Thirty minutes into the trip, three men passed her by. Over the years, Katrinka had developed an uncanny ability to sense something suspicious. Her curiosity now on alert, she made a mental note to keep an eye on them. There was a transfer at Konya for the final four hour and fifty-two-minute run to Istanbul. At Konya, she purchased two bottles of water, an energy bar, and something resembling a sandwich. All went into her pack.

People watching- one did that when their past life included intelligence gathering and espionage. The time had arrived for the train to depart. Katrinka verified she had the correct ticket for this leg of the trip. As she made her way to board her assigned car, three men pushed their way past her. The same guys.

****

10:45 A.M., the Sphinx

Fay and Azrael stood in awe of the huge lion with the man's head. From their vantage point, they could view not only the Sphinx but the pyramids of Giza behind it.

"Where do you suppose his nose went?" Fay wondered aloud.

Azrael was quickly proving herself to be quite the tour guide. "There are many Egyptian statues without noses," Azrael said. "It was believed the souls of the dead lived in the statues. The souls entered and exited the statues through their noses. Over the centuries, the idiots who occupied Egypt - Persians, Romans, and anyone else - defaced as many statues as they could find. Fortunately for history, they didn't get them all."

Fay and Azrael walked from the Sphinx toward the Great Pyramid.

"You have only a few friends. May I ask who they are?" Azrael inquired.

Fay thought for couple of seconds, as if she were organizing them in her mind. "Well," she said at last, "there would be my sister, my BFF. I call her JP because her name is Jansche Pearce. My mom and dad adopted her. Her mother was an American Indian, hence the Indian heritage given name. She met and married a Navy Sea captain. His name is Egan."

"Your sister sounds cool, Fay," Azrael remarked.

"She is one of a kind, as they say," Fay agreed. "And then there is Sasha. I met him on an aircraft carrier during a hearing involving a collision between Russian and American ships. We remained friends. Later, I had an assignment in Moscow. We met again. He introduced me to Katrinka and Irishka."

"Lady Katrinka and Irishka are both spies, aren't they?" Azrael guessed.

"Well, I suppose it is something that should remain confidential, but safe to say, they worked for Russian Naval intelligence," confirmed Fay.

"And Lady Katrinka began spy school when she was like thirteen or something?"

"Not at first," Fay corrected. "Later, she met Sasha and Irishka. They played a big part in moving her away from Russia and to the United States."

"Where you adopted her," Azrael said.

"That's right. She is legally now my daughter."

Azrael then said, "It is so impressive. Is there a special man?"

"It would depend on how you define 'special,' I suppose," Fay replied. She then asked, "Can we find a spot in the shade to sit for a spell? I seem to feel a bit tired."

The two women found a spot located on the shady side of a tour bus where they sat in the sand. Fay continued. "One guy is a Navy SEAL." She took a sip from her water bottle.

"Don't drink all of it, ma'am," Azrael advised. "It's going to get hotter later. You will need the water to dump on your head. It cools you off."

"For real? I pour it on my head?" Fay could tell Azrael was dead serious. "Okay, back to the SEAL," Fay said. "He was not a SEAL at the time I met him. He was, for lack of a better term, a hit man, for a really bad guy. The guy did not like me because I had busted him and his association for violations of anti-trust laws. And because he had a total dislike and lack of respect for all women. So, he had the hit man try to kill me."

Azrael brought her hands to her mouth. "Oh! But he didn't," Azrael said.

"It turned out this hit man had a heart. He and another guy had left me in the desert, along with my sister. The guy who ordered the hit had beaten me and told the hit man to leave us in the desert. To top it off, I had amnesia!" Fay told her.

"But you survived."

"I not only survived," Fay recalled, "but went on to send everyone involved in the anti-trust case to jail."

"What about the hit man?" Azrael asked.

"Jon is his name. He did not explain why he did not kill me," Fay recounted. "He told a man who became another friend of mine. Charlie, a Navajo Indian, rescued us. Jon later came to me to warn me that the guy who had hired him had sent another hit man kill me."

"This guy really hated you, didn't he?" Azrael remarked.

"As it turned out, I had a face-to-face with the guy. I was going to shoot him but Jon was worried about me. He knew I was going to meet with the man to exchange a list of names for my agreement to abandon the anti-trust prosecution." Fay went on, "The man attacked me, again. I shot in self-defense. I thought I had shot him, but later, I found out Jon had. So, Jon saved my life twice. He went back to the SEALs and he and I have since had two ops together. I call him my angel assassin."

"Ma'am, I am going to write a book on your life," Azrael teased.

Fay laughed. "You would not believe it, but there is much more. You sure you want to hear it?"

"Of course," Azrael replied. "Often and always."

****

Two hundred miles south of Istanbul, Turkey

The train made a scheduled stop. Katrinka knew she would have several minutes to stretch and catch a few breaths of fresh air. As she stood by the rail car, she saw the three men who had been traveling with her leave the train. They disappeared into the terminal building. The train's whistle sounded. All aboard.

****

1: 45 P.M., the Giza Plateau, Cairo, Egypt

Other than the bus, which eventually moved, shade was non-existent. A hat, sunglasses, and sunscreen were a fair skinned woman's only salvation. From the base of the Great Pyramid, Fay watched a small train of camels as they made their way from somewhere to somewhere else.

Azrael seemed to sense Fay's fascination with the beasts. "How about we rent two?" Azrael said, pointing toward a group of nearby sleepy camels. "You may never have this chance again."

Fay eagerly agreed.

"Let me do the talking," Azrael suggested. "These guys are scammers. They are super annoying. Especially if you refuse them anything. Don't let them take your picture in front of their camel. What happens is they promise a free picture then act offended if you turn them down. If you agree, they will want to take the picture with your cell. They hold your cell for ransom until you pay them for the photo." Azrael flashed a sly grin. "My foot up their ass usually fixes the problem," she informed Fay.

Azrael's matter-of-fact disclosure drew a hearty laugh from Fay. She waited while Azrael went to negotiate with the camel scammers. After a few minutes of finger pointing and what appeared to Fay to be arguing, Azrael returned with three camels and a camel jockey. "I will explain it to you later," she said.

The jockey pounded on the beasts and barked something at them in Arabic. Two of the camels lowered themselves to their knees. The man motioned for the women to climb aboard. He then jumped onto the remaining camel. He barked something else and the camels lurched to their feet. Had Fay not been hanging on, she would have found herself face down with a mouthful of sand when her camel lurched forward as he, or she, or it rose from its knees.

Fay asked, as she looked at what she could see of the great beast, and patted him/her/it on the head, "Do these things come with an operator's manual?"

Azrael laughed. "You sure are a lot of fun, ma'am!"

The tour, in the scorching sun, circled the Great Pyramid, affording Fay and Azrael a lot of photos from many angles. Part way, the scammer jockey stopped the small caravan. He hopped off his camel, ran across the burning sand to the pyramid, and then returned. He presented the women with two small chunks of stone.

"For my queens," he announced. "A piece of the pyramid. It is magical. You will have good luck and good fortune."

Fay was flattered by the "queen" part but also wondered if it might be illegal to possess a piece of antiquity. There had to be some law against it. By the time the tour ended, Fay was ready for it to be over. The women thanked the camel jockey, tipped him, and slowly walked, with bowed legs, toward their waiting car and driver. Fay felt for the poor driver. He had been waiting all afternoon, in the desert sun, for them to return.

Once inside the cool, airconditioned car, Fay asked, "What were you going to tell me about the camels?"

"I wanted you to know I was able to scam the scammers," Azrael responded.

"Oh," Fay replied. "Tell me more."

"These guys don't know the difference between an Arabic speaking Latino gal from East LA and an Egyptian from east Cairo," Azrael said. "I led them to believe I was your tour guide. The way the system works here is if a guide brings a tourist to a camel or any business, for that matter, the guide gets a twenty-five percent piece of the action. So, I give them the money and they unknowingly give me twenty-five percent of my money back to me. Slick, yes?"

"So, we just tipped the jockey with his own money. Slick!" Fay said.

Their driver, who had been listening, also got a good laugh out of Azrael's reverse scam.

Fay reassured him, "Don't worry, sir. We will pay you with our money."

****

6:02 P.M., Halkali Rail Station, Istanbul, Turkey

The evening train from Konya arrived on time. There would be a three-hour connection to the night train to Budapest. It was a bit humid. Katrinka walked from the station until she found what appeared to be a reasonable eating establishment. She ordered a burger, fries, and an iced tea. She found a relaxing spot under a nearby tree and ate. There were too many things to wonder about. How were Faya, Sasha, Irishka, Andrew, and Binky, her cat? Somewhere out there, two Ukrainian agents were on her tail and she was a long way from home and alone.

****

6:30 P.M., Sofitel Cairo, Nile El Gezirah

Fay met with Azrael and Sasha for dinner in the hotel's restaurant. There was much conversation as Fay and Azrael recounted their big adventure in the desert.

Fay's cell chimed. She did not recognize the number displayed on the screen. Realizing it could not possibly be a scam call, she answered. "Fay Green here."

"Miss Green, I am Annastasia. I have information for you about Lady Katrinka."

Fay's emotions, in one brief moment, went from joy to fear and back again. "I am here with her guardian, Sasha," Fay told the caller. "Can I put you on speaker?"

"Of course. I wanted to tell you that Lady Katrinka is good," Annastasia said. "She spent several days with me in Cyprus. Now she has left. She will be in touch. I knew you would be worried; is why I call. Goodbye."

"Wait!" Fay cried, but the woman was gone. Fay

clicked off the cell. Placing it on the table, she said, "I don't know what to think."

"She is alive and well, Faya," Sasha said. "We can hope for the best."

"Thank you for your words of encouragement, my friend." Fay sat back. "Wow. I worry so much. But now we know she is alive and will contact us."

"I know you worry about her," Sasha said. "You know she is an unusual girl, one who lived for ten years in the most dangerous conditions and survived it. If anyone can, she will survive this."

"I know, Sasha," Fay replied. "I just don't want her to suffer."

"Ma'am," Azrael said, "Lady Katrinka is what Sasha said. She is a tough, intimidating, and uncompromising badass. And she did escape from prison using only a pen."

****

8:20 P.M., Halkali Rail Station, Istanbul, Turkey

It was forty minutes until the night train to Budapest would depart. The 950-mile leg of her journey from Istanbul to Budapest would consume thirty-four and one-half hours of Kat's time. Fortunately, there was both a sleeping car and a dining car for this leg of the journey. About ten minutes before her departure, a curiosity presented itself. The three guys, the ones who had left the train two hundred miles back, boarded the night train. A large "huh" formed in Katrinka's now curious mind. At the same time, she reminded herself, it was curiosity that killed the Kat.

Her challenge was to both sleep and keep an eye on the three men. She made her way to her berth, where she stowed her pack. Katrinka studied the train schedule, noting the arrival times at each stop. Knowing the three mystery men would not be dumb enough to jump from the train until they had returned their tray tables to their full and upright positions and until the train came to a full and complete stop, she would sleep and then watch for their possible unboarding. Throughout the night, her scheme worked like a charm. During the day, it was easy for her to monitor the suspicious guys.

****

5:34 P.M., a railway station of Videle, Romania

From a sightseeing point of view, the journey past rivers, farms, lakes, and through mountain passes were the stuff travel promotions and movies scenes were made of. During the twenty-four-minute stop at Videle station, Katrinka took the opportunity to find a newspaper, a bottle of spring water, and a packet of cigarettes. She did not smoke, never had; yet, the three guys spent a lot of time in the smoking car. If she wanted to get a closer look at them, or observe their suspicious natures, a cigarette was the price of admission.

The train left on time to begin its 14 hour and 56-minute trek to Budapest. Once the train was under way and she was reassured the three guys were not going to jump off, Katrinka stopped in the dining car for a light dinner. Heavy dinners could induce sleep, which she could not afford. Following dinner, she headed for the smoking car with her newspaper and pack of cigarettes in tow.

Reading and observing was a bit of multitasking that often paid off when one was in the midst of intelligence gathering. Conversely, if one did not smoke, it was hard to pretend that one did. Coughing was usually a giveaway. Katrinka read, observed, and worked hard to stifle a cough here and there, but the headlines eventually succeeded in drawing a cough from her lungs. One item in particular caught her attention: a photo and a story. The French Embassy, two hundred miles south of Istanbul, had been rocked by a small explosion. No one thus far had taken credit for the bombing. Three bombings in three cities had occurred on the same days she had visited each place. What a coincidence.

Chapter 7

9:45 A.M., Sofitel, Cairo, Nile El Gezirah

Fay and Azrael sat in what had become their favorite eating and meeting place, the Bar Lounge on the Nile. The two women ordered breakfast. Meanwhile, Fay scanned the French language version of the local newspaper. She had looked high and low for an English paper. Beside her, Azrael caught up on her texts.

"Mom says she is worried about me. Yeah, and I know how mothers worry," Azrael said, pointing in Fay's direction. "She and Dad hope I can visit soon, but they know duty to God and country comes first." She was silent. Azrael then said, "Here is one from First Sergeant. He says another French Embassy was bombed." She continued to scan the text. "This time in Istanbul."

Fay remained silent.

"Ma'am, if Lady Katrinka is heading north, as we suppose, it seems the bombings are following her," Azrael observed.

Fay texted Sasha: *Are you coming for breakfast?*

A familiar voice from behind her said, "I am almost there."

Fay turned, smiled and said, "Morning, Sasha. Your timing is perfect. Azrael said there was another embassy bombing, this one at the French Embassy in Istanbul."

"I know what you are thinking," Sasha immediately replied. "I assure you, Katrinka is okay and doing what she has been trained to do. She is as feral as any cat when relying on her instincts."

"I have a hard time comparing our Kat to a wild cat," Fay responded, "but I do understand your analogy. Much appreciated, my friend."

"What's on the agenda today?" asked Sasha.

"Azrael and I are headed for the museum to view Tut's, pardon the pun, death head mask," Fay informed him. "Wanna come with?"

"Two lovely women? Lots of gold? How can I resist?" Sasha stood and continued, "If I am to go, I have something to attend to. Meet you back here?"

"How about an hour from now?" Fay asked.

"See you then, ladies."

Azrael watch Sasha as he walked away. "He is really a cool guy," she observed.

Fay agreed. "Beyond cool."

"You were telling me about your friends," Azrael reminded Fay. "We had made it to special friends. We had left off at the assassin."

"Okay," Fay acknowledged. "There is another guy. He was a sheriff in Florida. A Navy admiral was murdered. I found his body and the sheriff took over the investigation because I had to go to a meeting in Quantico, where I met you."

"Fate, ma'am," Azrael remarked. "Go on."

"Over time, his investigation overlapped with the anti-trust case I was involved in," remembered Fay. "He became a witness and had to go into federal witness protection. I only see glimpses of him from time to time."

"That is downright sad, Fay. Did you ever see your friend the assassin again?" Azrael asked.

"Twice more. One time, we ran an op in Czech Republic. It involved freeing American young women from human trafficking. The other time …" Fay paused. "The other time I cannot talk about."

"Sorry I asked."

"No. No. It's that I don't remember it," Fay stated. "The reason is classified."

"The most exciting thing that ever happened to me was I actually graduated from high school," Azrael said. "And the Marines allowed me to join up."

"After all that has happened to me over the past three years, I would gladly trade you," Fay assured the other woman.

"And there is more to tell. Right?" Azrael guessed.

"Yep. The best part is yet to come. I will tell you about it tonight," Fay promised. "In the meantime, let's get our butts over to see Tut and friends."

****

8:56 A.M., Budapest Keleti (Eastern) Railway Station (Hungarian: Keleti pályaudvar)

It was Kat's habit to practice the age-old fable: look before you leap. During two minutes of looking, she spotted not only the two Ukrainian lads but Inspector Popov as well. Everyone seemed to be looking for her. She had yet to determine why the topknots were following her. But there they were. Popov and the topknots' political differences would not be conducive to a partnership. The last time she had seen Popov was at the Moscow airport. She, in so many words, had told him she was his other prime suspect in the assassination of Evilenko, a man who had been hired to kill her Faya. Evilenko had been shot in broad daylight in a crowded Moscow Arbat bar. Popov's jurisdiction apparently extended beyond Russian borders. Probably Interpol?

Katrinka paused for a moment to text Nastasya at the Russian Embassy in Cyprus. She hoped she would get the message: *Istanbul...help...Russian Embassy.* She gathered her pack and departed from the train.

Her plan was to follow the three men, ensuring Popov and the topknots saw her and followed her. Katrinka needed to stay ahead of Popov, not to lose him, but to keep pace with the three guys she was following. Her plan had significant risks assigned to it. Her assumption was the men were headed for the French Embassy. She knew if she stopped at any point before she reached her destination, Popov would catch up with her and most likely arrest her. Her plan was clever, if her assumption was correct. If not, what may well prove to the grandest shit-show since the Trump-Clinton presidential debate of years past would ensue.

When Katrinka arrived at the embassy and was sure the three suspects had stopped there as well, she took up a position under the shade of a tree across the street from the embassy. Her hope now was it did not take Popov too long to catch up. Her surveillance was focused on the three men.

From behind her she heard a voice say, "Miss Lavrova."

Katrinka turned immediately, bringing her index finger to her lips. Then she pointed to a lone man now standing holding a backpack, off to the side of the embassy gate. She said to Popov, "Troye muzhchin. Bum!" *("Three men. Boom!")*

Inspector Popov had a choice. Believe her and run to stop the impending explosion. Or not believe her and arrest her, and then tend to an explosion later. He briefly considered his options.

Kat must have had established enough credibility with him. He said, "Paka, paka. Go."

Kat did not wait to chat. She turned and sprinted the one and one-half miles to the Russian Embassy, while hoping, as she ran, that Annastasia had received her text and alerted the embassy she might be by for a visit. She did not hear an explosion. Either Popov and his man had thwarted the attack, or he was not standing in front of the French Embassy with *oeuf* on his face.

Kat was running so fast, she almost ran past the Embassy. A small course correction put her at the main gate. An embassy guard met her there. She pushed her passport through the bars. The guard scanned it. And good luck shined on her that day. The guard opened the gate, admitting her to the embassy. She had another dose of fortune: the guard was a woman, so no extended pat down was required.

In Russian, the guard said, "Welcome to Embassy of Russian Federation. Please proceed through door." She pointed toward the Embassy's main entrance.

As she passed by the guard, Kat mentioned there were likely two topknots lurking across the street. The guards, now aware, would deal with them in their own way.

****

Sofitel, Cairo, Nile El Gezirah

Fay requested and was granted an extended

emergency leave of absence for thirty days. All she and Sasha could do was wait for word from Irishka or Katrinka. Irishka was in contact with Sasha on a regular basis. They knew Kat was traveling by train, making her way to Paris. Sasha said now would be the time for them to relocate to Paris. Fay, with Azrael's approval, asked her own boss, JAG Captain Vern Towsley, if he would pull whatever strings he could to have Corporal Lopez given a temporary duty assignment to the Navy as her A.A. Towsley was able to push the request through.

Fay booked a Paris-bound Air France flight, departing in the evening, for Sasha, Azrael, and herself. The hotel staff booked rooms for them at the Sofitel Paris Baltimore Tour Eiffel Hotel. Sasha planned to stay only two days then return to Moscow, knowing Katrinka would be secure in a Russian safe house. Even though Fay did not know the location of the safe house, she was comforted by knowing she was at least in proximity to Katrinka. There was hope they would reunite soon.

****

7:40 A.M., Budapest Keleti (Eastern) Railway Station

The Railjet left the Budapest station for the two hour and forty minute journey to Vienna. The total time to Paris would be fourteen hours and forty-five minutes. Katrinka saw neither Popov nor the topknots at the station, although she reasoned Popov had gotten himself deep into a mound of paperwork. She chuckled when she read the headlines in the *Budapest Times.* Interpol had apprehended three suspects for the attempted bombing of the French Embassy in Budapest and two other French Embassy bombings. The *kloun* would probably get a promotion and a raise in pay for all of his hard work in cracking the "hit and run embassy bombers" case.

Popov was out of her hair for the time being and she had not seen the topknots this morning. Katrinka picked up a cup of coffee from the coffee vendor and sat to rest her brain. Her thoughts drifted time and again to the Ukrainian agents - the topknots. Even though they seemed to be following her, she thought it odd they only appeared randomly. Nor did they seem aggressive. Her first awareness of the topknots had been at the dock when she had arrived in Cyprus. Later, only occasionally did they resurface as she had traveled to Budapest. They seemed to know where she was and when. What did they want from her? They did not seem like they had any intention of killing her. But maybe they did.

It was troubling, until something occurred to her. Katrinka grabbed her pack and moved to a secluded portion of the train. Emptying the contents of the pack onto an adjoining seat, she examined each item. Her search proved fruitless, but a thought kept nagging at her. Her eyes settled on a rolled pair of socks. Inside the roll, she had placed a Swiss Army knife She unrolled the socks, opened the knife, and cut into one of the pack's shoulder straps. She found what she was looking for, a tracking device - as well as something she was not looking for, a cloth bag. She felt the bag: small rocks. She did not have to open the bag. They were gems. She cut open the other strap. Another bag, more rocks.

Katrinka stuffed the bags back into the straps,

along with the tracking device. If she hoped to see the topknots again, she had to help them find her. Apparently, she had inadvertently become someone's mule and jewel smuggler. The Ukrainians? She returned to her assigned seat for the remainder of the journey.

Faya always said, "Can of worms," whatever that meant. The little rocks were more curious than the tracking device. With the tracking device, she could keep track of the topknots. Reverse tracking, if you will. At what point in her journey from Cairo up until now had she inherited both the can and the worms? The topknots may have more interest in the rocks than they did in her. If the rocks were conflict diamonds, as she suspected, it might suggest the diamonds were payment to the Ukrainians in exchange for weapons sold to a warring African nation. Libya was Egypt's western neighbor and it was a warring African nation.

By the time the Railjet arrived at Paris Gar du Nord, the busiest railway station in Europe, it was 10:45 P.M. Her rest stop was the safe house. It was yet to be determined where she would stash the pack. Unless she removed the tracking device, she would lead the topknots to the safe house. The defensive safe house was within walking distance of the train station. Her best option was to leave the pack in a locker. Then, after confirming she had not attracted a trail, Katrinka set out for the safe house. She executed several maneuvers designed to lose a trail. No one would be able to follow her to the safe house.

It was 11:30 P.M. when Kat checked into the small, out of the way, older hotel on Rue Bervic. The room was adequate: a small main floor apartment with a bath, a phone, and a small color TV. For a safe house to be spy efficient, it needed to be easy to get into and out of, with a quick exit in the event one was discovered and needed to avoid capture. The room's location near the busy railway station and pedestrian traffic allowed her to blend into a crowd. A heavy curtain on the single window would make it easier to watch the hotel entrance. Katrinka found a makeshift doorless safe behind the only picture hung on the wall. A cell phone and a battery were stored within. The phone would be set on airplane mode to discourage tracing. The hole in the wall was a good place to hide a weapon, documents, or diamonds.

Katrinka showered and redressed for bed. When one was in hiding, it was best to sleep in clothing designed for immediate departure, sometimes including shoes. All and all, it was frowned upon for a lady spy to make an emergency departure from her room in pajamas and fluffy leopard print slippers. She had not eaten. There was an open bistro across the street where she purchased a loaf of bread, bottles of water, a small bottle of wine, and a piece of jerky.

****

07:45 A.M., Paris, Charles de Gaulle Airport (Aéroport de Paris-Charles-de-Gaulle Roissy Airport)

Fay, Sasha, and Azrael made their way to baggage claim. Fay's cell chimed. She stepped aside to allow those passengers walking behind her to continue toward baggage claim. The caller ID indicated "Unknown." She knew it to be Irishka. The text was cryptic: *Kitten with mother.*

Fay smiled. She clicked off the phone and said to Azrael and Sasha, "Lady K is with us in Paris."

Thirty-four kilometers away, Katrinka sat at a small table at one of Paris's many sidewalk cafes, eating a typical Parisian breakfast consisting of a croissant, tartine, café au lait, and juice. Ever vigilant for anything out of the ordinary, she had been contemplating for thirty minutes or so the cell which had been left for her in the safe house by Irishka, or someone associated with the management of the safe house. The temptation to call was too strong, yet the potential exposure to tracking was something to be cautious about. The phone was standard issue spy gear. A prepaid model set in airplane mode would be hard to trace. Temptation won out.

Fay's cell chimed. Again, the caller was "Unknown." "Fay," she answered.

"Hi, mama. It's me, Kat."

Fay, who normally reserved her screams for major lotto wins, screamed.

"Mama...are you okay?" Kat asked.

"My sweet girl! You are okay!" Fay exclaimed.

"I am fine," Kat reassured her. "But I only have short minute. I want you to know I am in Paris. I am in safe house. Irishka helps me. Are you good?"

"Yes. Yes. Yes...I'm good. When will we see you?" Fay asked.

"When I am done. I will call. Tell angel I buy her new pen when I see her. I must go. *Paka paka*." And Katrinka was gone.

Fay wondered if she would make it to baggage claim in one piece. Screams emitted in airports tended to attract a lot of unwanted attention, included airport security.

Chapter 8

After shopping for beer and wine and several unimported items, plus food and a magazine, Katrinka walked to the train station. The station was busy, but the crowd count was manageable. One of the spy schools had taught her large groups of people proved to be as good a place to hide as a forest. After fifteen minutes of observing the locker, she felt reassured the topknots, or anyone else, were not surveilling it. With caution, Katrinka approached the locker and withdrew the pack. She extracted the bags of rocks and stuffed the pack, with the tracking device remaining inside, back into the locker. Her return trip to the safe house followed the same procedure as before. If anyone were following her, they were now looking for her a mile away.

Katrinka knew where she had acquired the pack. It was on loan from a tourist she had not meet near Alexandra. There was a label indicating the gal's name and address. One day, the value of the pack twenty times over would be mailed to her, along with an apology. But where Kat had inherited the diamonds remained a mystery.

Katrinka cut into a bag using her pocketknife. She found the little scissors feature handy; the bottle opener was also another useful feature. She opened a bottle of Popihn Russian Imperial Stout v.3. The nice fellow at the market had recommended the brew and had promised it was one of France's most popular. "*Magnifique*," was his exact word. The first sip proved him right.

Using scissors, she cut the bags, emptying the rocks onto a table. The rocks appeared to be colorful diamonds. She was not an expert. Katrinka found her cell in a small satchel she had purchased at a shop near the hotel. After inserting the battery, she took six photos of the stones. She removed the battery from the cell, scooped the stones back into the bags, and placed the bags into the satchel.

****

9:40 A.M., Paris, Baltimore Tour Eiffel Hotel

After Fay and friends checked in and were shown to their rooms, Fay asked if they would meet her in one of the hotel's bars. After receiving the call from Kat, as she put it, "My nerves are shot. Would one of you mind helping me unwind?"

Sasha and Azrael both offered. Drinks, hopefully mimosas, more than two, were the objects of Fay's desire.

Azrael had never been to Paris. East LA, Cairo, Quantico, and basic training at Parris Island, a different Paris all together, were the extent of her travel portfolio. Fay did not recall seeing anyone whose eyes were as large as Azrael's.

"Ma'am, I have two latrines in my room," Azrael informed her incredulously.

Fay responded, "One is called a bidet. I will fill you in later."

"Cool!" she chirped.

Sasha asked, "Should we order brunch?"

"Please, y'all should eat," Fay told him. "I am going to drink my brunch." Fay's cell chimed. A text from "Unknown" alerted her to six messages: six photos of what appeared to her to be colorful diamonds. Nothing more. She handed the phone to Azrael, who shrugged and then passed it on to Sasha.

Sasha examined each photo twice. "Colorful diamonds," he replied. "Just the photos?"

"Do you think Kat sent them?" Fay asked

"Who else, Faya?" Sasha told her.

Fay stopped a waiter as he passed by their table, "Je vous demande pardon," she said.

The waiter answered, "Óui, mademoiselle comment puis-je-alder. Tiffany and Company. Just up the street, mademoiselle," the waiter replied. "Away from the river."

Sasha said, "Why don't you ladies visit Tiffany while I visit Russian Embassy?"

Fay called the waiter to the table. "Monsieur, vas-tu mettre ca dans notre chambre?"

Azrael smiled at the waiter and watched him walk away from the table. "Cute guy," she said. "What did you say to him, ma'am?"

"I asked him to charge the drinks to my room," Fay told her.

"Thank you, ma'am. How many languages do you speak, Fay?" Azrael inquired.

"French, Italian, some Russian, and a little English," Fay said. "How about you?"

Azrael giggled. "You speak English fine. Me...I speak Arabic, Spanish, Chicano English, and Valley Girl."

"Is Valley Girl considered a language, Azrael?"

Fay teased.

"So, um, I'm like 'Where did the waiter go?' and you're um, like, 'I don't know, I like don't know,'" Azrael joked.

Fay smiled. "Well said, girlfriend. So, let's um, like, let's go. And when we like, um, get back, we can like watch *Clueless.* 'Kay?"

Azrael laughed and slapped her thigh. "Someday, I hope you visit me in LA. You will fit right in," she declared.

Their stroll along Avenue Kleber was invigorating. Yet, Fay again experienced mild exhaustion. Fay and her doctor knew why. She chose to keep the reasons to herself.

"Bonjour Bon matin," the Tiffany associate welcomed Fay and Azrael.

"*Bonjour,*" Fay replied. "Thank you. We are here to meet for an appraisal."

"Of course, mademoiselle." The associate motioned toward a nearby lounge. "If you will make yourselves comfortable, I will find someone for you. Would you care for a latte?"

"*Merci.* We would," Fay replied.

The kid from East LA was awestruck. "Ma'am, will they let me take photos?" Azrael whispered.

"I think it will be okay."

Azrael spotted a life size black and white likeness of someone who apparently had celebrity status. She moved near the likeness. "Who is it, ma'am?" she asked.

"Her name is Audrey Hepburn," Fay said. "She was an actor. A long time ago, there was a famous romantic movie filmed here called *Breakfast at*

Tiffany's. Every woman, and some guys, loved the movie."

Azrael had been busy searching the internet while Fay spoke. "Wow," Azrael said. "Audrey Hepburn is so elegant. You know, she reminds me of Lady Kat."

"I can see it," Fay agreed, "at least from the elegance point of view."

"Can we take a selfie, Fay?" Azrael requested.

Fay and Azrael stood next to Audrey for several photo ops.

"In the film, her character was Holly Golightly," Fay explained.

"Cool name. Pretty woman," Azrael agreed as she took another selfie.

"If you want to look at the jewelry, I'll wait for the appraisal," Fay offered.

A kid in a candy store would best describe Fay's assessment of Azrael and her excitement, as she perused the cases of beyond-expensive jewelry.

Ten minutes passed. A gentleman entered the lounge. Spotting Fay, his eyes lit up. "*Bonjour, Bonjour*. Welcome to Tiffany's," he said.

"*Merci*," Fay replied.

"I am Mourad. How can I be of service, *mademoiselle*? May I sit?"

"Of course. Thank you for seeing me," she replied. "I am Faydra Green."

"Not a problem for you," Mourad responded.

Fay clicked on her cell. "I have photos of some stones, I believe gems, but I am looking for an opinion." She handed the cell to him.

Mourad was cell phone savvy. Fay remained silent while he scrolled back and forth between photos, enlarging a few as he did so. "It is so difficult to say, Faydra," Mourad finally said. "I can tell you they are uncut diamonds. But, of course, you knew it." He reviewed the photos again. He pointed to one photo and showed her. "These colorful ones are possibly of value. They appear to be blue in their color. However, they all may be the same. I do not know."

"I understand I am asking the impossible, Mourad. Can you tell me anything?" Fay inquired.

Mourad asked, "Can you bring me these stones?"

"I may be able to."

"It would be best. But I can safely say if these are blue, as they appear, and I believe them to be perhaps two carats or more, if so, then for the twenty-four..." Mourad appeared to make a mental calculation. "Perhaps two to three million each? Maybe more?" he estimated.

"Mercy. They are of a rarer variety then?" Fay asked.

"The colors, the blue, the red, the pinks...are most desirable. We have them but they are most expensive," Mourad stated. "I can say, on behalf of Tiffany and Company, we would have an interest in these gems. Will you consider us if you should decide to sell?" Mourad drew a card from his jacket pocket. "My card."

Fay accepted his card. Years of education and training had taught her to review the card, rather than simply stuff it into her pocket. "Thank you, Mourad." Fay glanced to see where Azrael was. "Would you have a salesperson help us?"

"Mademoiselle, I am at your exclusive disposal," Mourad replied. "What may I show you?"

"I would like to buy a souvenir for my friend to

commemorate her visit to Tiffany's," Fay informed him.

"Something simple, but not too expensive? Yet true to the Tiffany tradition?" Mourad guessed.

"Perfect." Fay got Azrael's attention. She motioned for Azrael to join them.

Azrael approached the two people with a broad smile on her face.

"*Bonjour*," Mourad said to Azrael.

"Azrael, this is Mourad," Fay said in introduction. "He is going to help us find a souvenir. Do you want to help us?"

"Can I?" Azrael replied.

Fay said, "Show us what you like."

"I already know, ma'am. I knew I had to have something," Azrael told them. "I calculated how much I had in my savings account. Something I can afford."

"Show us," Fay eagerly encouraged her.

Azrael had found a simple, small diamond cross necklace.

Mourad went behind the case to remove the cross. The necklace was displayed on a black velvet plate. Mourad slipped on a pair of white gloves then handed the necklace to Azrael. He moved a small mirror and held it for her to see the necklace as she held it near her neck. She modeled it for Fay.

"Perfect. It is you," Fay said.

"I agree," Mourad said. "It is most exquisite."

Azrael smiled. "Can I use my credit card?" she inquired.

"Of course, mademoiselle," Mourad replied.

Azrael's hands trembled as she searched her purse for her card. In the meantime, Fay had handed her

American Express to Mourad. When Azrael had found her card, she then noticed Mourad already had a card.

"Ma'am, I cannot let you," Azrael protested. "No. Please," she pleaded.

Mourad excused himself.

Fay said, "If for no other reason, this is for you for loaning your pen to Katrinka. But it is not the reason. You have been a mega help to me since we met. I want to offer something to you as a token of my gratitude."

****

Hanging around in a safehouse was boring. A small color TV featured programs offered in a language she did not understand. A bottle of beer, a magazine or two, and, if she got lucky, a bird landed on the windowsill or a mouse found its way into her bathroom. Katrinka was not the screaming type, rodents were commonplace, yet she felt obliged to squash the germ ridden little pest. For short stints, she searched online using her cell, looking up things like "how to speak French in just three days," or "BBC." She finally reached the point of madness. To break the monotony, it was time to go somewhere. The *Rive Gauche* was a great place to people watch. With boats full of nonproductive tourists cruising by, it was a good place to keep an eye on the Eiffel Tower. It was a place where everyone looked like a Frenchie, and if a Ukrainian spy or two were to show up, one could jump into the river and escape. *Rive Gauche* was a wonderful place to have a picnic and to tan your pale skin, and it was within walking distance of her now mouse free home.

Katrinka wondered, off and on, what to do with the expensive little stones. The river was a depository option to be considered. Yet, perhaps a few of those pesky little gypsy beggars' kids who frequented everywhere there was a flock of tourists to be found could make use of them. Although to hand a kid a rock which may well be worth a million dollars and have them understand how it could make their life better would be challenging. Katrinka did wonder why the people of France seemed to not care to speak English like the little gypsy kids did. French indifference played a part, she was certain of it. Faya would know what to do with the rocks, but then again Faya possessing the rocks could draw unwanted attention to her. Irishka? No. The Russian government? Let them deal with it. The usual outcome would enable several more oligarchs. Someone at the U.S. Embassy? But then again, the U.S. has a bad habit of losing things of higher value or simply spending them to buy large amounts of nothing. If someone would have once told her two pocketfuls of diamonds would be a problem, she would have not believed them.

Katrinka had not yet concluded where she had obtained her problems to begin with. Like the mouse, they had just shown up. She had likely acquired them during her stay at the Russian Embassy in Cyprus. She had first spotted the topknots on her arrival at the dock in Cyprus. Her borrowed pack had only been out of her sight when she had attended the party at the Embassy in Cyprus. The topknots seemed content to follow her but not engage with her. It now occurred to her she may have misidentified the topknots. Russian surveillance agents did appear very similar in manner of dress and stature to their Ukrainian counterparts.

Katrinka had been given the rocks for safekeeping. Those who had given them to her would, at some point, expect them back. If she tossed them in the river, they would feel compelled to have her retrieve them. She considered Sasha and Irishka as an option. Sasha was Russian, a tough guy, a decent spy, knew people in the Kremlin, and worst of all, he was a lawyer. Irishka and Wonder Spy Woman were one in the same, in Katrinka's mind. She respected Fay's advice. She would text Fay, meet her, and have her promise not to scream this time. Screams tended to attract the kind of attention she least desired, for the moment.

Katrina removed her spy cell from her satchel and texted Fay with a heart emoji greeting.

Fay messaged back: *R U O K?*

Katrinka chuckled at the off-the-cuff code system. It was corny code but worked for her. Katrinka messaged: *Yes, I am K. Tomorrow, Louvre, noon, I will find you. And bring Marines. Ciao.*

For the first time in more than a month, Katrinka experienced a measure of joy in her heart. The Louvre was a big place with lots of people. Another good place to hide. Granted, it would take work to find Fay and Azrael. Near the glass pyramid entry around noon would be the most logical place to begin her search.

Across town, Fay contained her excitement. "Katrinka will meet us tomorrow at noon," she told Azrael.

"I am so happy for you both, ma'am," Azrael replied. "We should celebrate with lunch, drinks, and cute waiters in the hotel restaurant."

Chapter 9

Louvre Museum, Paris, France

As secretive as a recluse spider, Katrinka watched as Fay and Azrael entered the glass pyramid and disappeared down the escalator. She waited five minutes before she too entered the Louvre. Once she had purchased her admission, she moved quickly into the museum. She reasoned everyone and their brother would be viewing the Mona Lisa. It would be a good place for her to hide. The portrait would be her best chance to locate Fay in the massive museum.

Eventually, Fay and Azrael found their way to the portrait of the Mona Lisa. The viewing area was crowded, with all in attendance jockeying for an up-close chance to get a piece of Leonardo da Vinci's grand masterpiece. Katrinka waited until Fay moved on to an almost vacant grand master's viewing gallery. Most of the paintings were larger than Fay's garage door. Her intention was to first speak to Azrael in private. She waited until Fay had left Azrael alone.

As Kat approached Azrael, it seemed to her Azrael was expecting to see her at that moment. "Hello," Katrinka greeted her. "Nice to meet you again."

Azrael returned Katrinka's greeting in Russian. "Hello, Lady Katrinka. Come. Sit with me," she said in welcome.

The two women continued their conversation in the Russian language. "I wanted to speak to you alone," Katrinka said. "Fay will return soon." Katrinka reached into her satchel and withdrew a pen. Offering it to Azrael, she said, "I return pen. I no use it." She smiled. "But you know it."

Azrael returned the smile.

"As I say before," Katrinka went on, "I would like to speak to you before Faya comes back."

"Fay will be a while. She went to the ladies' room and then she is going to get confused and turned around before she finds her way back to us," Azrael predicted.

"Then I am correct," Kat claimed. "You are more than Marine Embassy guard."

Azrael nodded, yes, but remained silent.

"Azrael, Angel of Death," Katrinka continued, "the psychopomp, who transports souls to afterlife after they die."

"Go on," Azrael coaxed.

"Two men follow me are not espionage agents but angels?" Katrinka asked.

Azrael offered her a confirming nod.

Katrinka's mood saddened. "You have purpose," she said. "I fear you are here to take my Faya to afterlife."

"That is what I like about you, Lady K. You are a badass and you are quick on the uptake," Azrael said.

"What do I do?" Katrinka asked.

"I like living as a human sometimes. I am not in a hurry to do my job. But I will when the time comes. In the meantime, I have grown to like your Faya," Azrael informed her. "She has a pure soul. They are very hard to find these days. I may be willing to negotiate,"

Azrael offered. "A soul for a soul?"

"Deal," Katrinka was quick to reply. "My soul for her soul."

The conversation returned to English. Azrael seemed to consider Katrinka's offer. "I'll think about it," she said. "But I may have something else in mind. Anyway, Fay will be back soon. We can talk later."

Shortly after, there was an echo in the hall. "There you two are!" Fay said, louder than she had intended. In an instant, she hugged Katrinka. Then the mush began to flow. "Oh. I am so happy to see you!" Fay exclaimed. "I have been so worried." Fay stepped back from Katrinka. "You are okay. You look good!" Fay continued, "Katrinka, you know Azrael."

Katrinka responded, "Azrael and I have had some time to get to know each other."

Fay apologized, "All I did was go to the ladies' room. Then, I got completely turned around and ended up somewhere else. Me! I never get lost."

Katrinka responded, "I wish I had time to visit but I must return to safe house. I cannot be out too long."

Katrinka could see the disappointment in Fay's expression. "I need help to leave France," Katrinka continued. "But I do not know my options. U.S. or Russia. Is it possible?"

"We have a lawyer in Cairo," Fay told her. "I will contact him to learn if the Egyptian government has placed a warrant for your arrest. Once we know the answer, Sasha and I will know if we need to begin extradition applications or not." Fay hugged Katrinka again. "It is so good to know you are alive and well, sweetheart."

"It is the same with me," Katrinka replied warmly.

"Can I do anything else for you?" Fay asked.

"Yes. The photo of stones I text to you," Katrinka said. "What about them?"

"They are a rarer blue diamond variety," Fay told her. "An appraiser at Tiffany thought them worth perhaps twenty to twenty-five million. But if they are conflict diamonds then I do not know."

"Thank you, Faya." The two women hugged again. "I will message you," Katrinka said. "I must go." Katrinka reached out to grasp Azrael's hand. "We can discuss."

Azrael nodded. "Take care, Lady Kat."

****

Katrinka returned from the nearby market with apples and beer. She flopped onto the bed and clicked on the TV. The guy at the front desk had given her a converter which allowed her to access a few English programs. They were mostly old American and British produced reruns, but they were all new to her. She found American humor odd, but the British humor was hard for her to appreciate. Television watching was boring, yet she found whatever the offering was, it caused her to fall asleep.

Sleep was about to claim her when a soft knock came at the door. Only the manager, or Irishka, knew she was there. Now fully awake and alert, Katrinka reached for her weapon and paused, listening for any telltale sound that might cause her concern.

"Katrinka," a voice called.

Kat knew the voice. It may be a friend. The jury was still out on her assessment of the person. She moved with caution to the door. She took the precaution of standing beside the door, and not in front of it, in case someone shot through the door so that she would not be in line with a bullet or three.

Deciding she had enough trust in the person on the opposite side, Kat unlatched the security chain and opened the door. At least the woman was smiling, the sign of a good beginning. "Azrael." Kat welcomed the visitor without surprise evident in her voice. "Come in."

Azrael proceed through the door as Kat closed it behind her.

Azrael surveyed the room. "Nice place. Fit for a queen," she said.

"Yeah. Right," Kat replied. "You want beer?"

"Sure!"

Kat retrieved a bottle from the refrigerator, opened the top with her pocketknife, then handed it to Azrael. "Have seat," she offered. "We talk."

Azrael sipped the beer. She smiled and looked at the bottle. "Beer over the centuries has greatly improved. The piss they served five hundred years ago was pathetic. Carbonation is the secret," Azrael said. She took a second sip.

Katrinka replied, "I would imagine many things have improved over the millennia."

"True," Azrael agreed. "Except for humans. All was going well until Gen Y came along. No offence."

"None taken." Katrinka pressed, "What of the deal you suggested?"

"Oh, yeah, yeah," Azrael said. "I almost forgot. There was a reason I came to see you."

With some doubt evident on her face, Katrinka reminded the forgetful Angel of Death, "The soul for a soul. Me for Faya."

Azrael's face brightened. "The deal. Well, I have

been thinking about it."

Katrinka became worried. Was Azrael going back on the offer? "Me for Faya. That was the offer," she stated firmly.

Azrael smiled. She took another sip of beer. "Great drink," she said. "I have another offer for you. You probably won't like it but hear me out."

Katrinka continued speaking to Lady Death in the Russian language. "You speak my language well."

"I'm not one to brag. Well, yes, I am one to brag," Azrael replied. "I'm fluent in over ten million languages," she boasted, "give or take."

Katrinka began to grow impatient. "The deal?" she prompted.

Azrael looked at Katrinka. "You wouldn't happen to have a cigar, would you?" she asked.

Katrinka's eyes lit up. "No, but I do have a cigarette."

Azrael shook her head, no. "I don't touch the stuff."

Katrinka now reasoned if she could keep Azrael's mind off of the deal, she may well forget about it. Again.

But no. "I told you, and you figured out some on your own," Azrael said. "Well played on that one, by the way."

"*Spacibo*," Kat replied.

Azrael continued, "My original intention was to claim Fay's soul. It was her time. And, the truth be known, she was well past her time. By all rights, she should have drowned on the mission a few years ago there in the Yellow Sea. But the dolphins got in the way and saved her."

"She told me," Kat recalled. "It was awesome."

"Then she outwitted an alligator and a shark, at the same time," Azrael explained. "That one impressed me."

"Me too."

"Then there was the sick bastard, Roman Justine. I hold Mazikim completely responsible for that wretch Justine trying to kill her, I think it was twice?" Azrael pondered. "Maybe three times? She outwitted him every time. She got him in the end."

"She has a knack for ducking death, it would seem," Kat observed.

"Yes," Azrael agreed. "However, this time is unavoidable."

"Why?"

Azrael revealed, "Fay has cancer. It will only get worse."

"I did not know it," Kat said sadly.

"She has told no one," Azrael replied. "She keeps it to herself. But this is the Fay I have come to know and to admire. You see, she has a pure heart. Those are very rare in humans. You know it, Lady K."

"She will give everything to anyone before she will give to herself," Kat stated.

"True. I have come to know her and to appreciate her," Azrael responded. "As a result, I am willing to deal. But a soul is required."

"A soul for a soul is what you said," Kat recounted.

"Fay's cancer is becoming painful for her. She hides it from all. Only her and her doctor know. And me," Azrael added.

"What can be done?" Kat wondered.

"If you and I strike a bargain, then tomorrow her

pain will subside," Azrael told Kat. "Her cancer will disappear, and she will live out her life, and well she should."

"Okay. I am in," Kat immediately replied. "But you say deal changed. You want more?"

"You, my dear Lady, have something I want," Azrael informed Kat. "You are also a rare human. You are a survivor, and you are clever. No one else would have experienced your life from age thirteen until now and have lived."

"I sometimes wonder it myself." Katrinka noticed Azrael's bottle was empty. "Can I get you another beer?" she offered.

"Please."

Katrinka retrieved a beer for Azrael, and encouraged her, "Please. Continue."

"We have the opportunity to right wrongs which have occurred in Russia since before the time of Tsar Nicholas II," Azrael went on. "Again, Mazikim screwed the pooch. Her guys were Rasputin and Lenin. Again, they are all on her. Always, this is Mazikim. Always trouble with that one."

"The deal is I agree to assume the headship of Russia as Princess Yekaterina, with you as my Rasputin," Kat guessed.

"Almost," Azrael corrected. "I want nothing to do with it. You would be on your own. You can handle it."

"What would be the purpose?" Kat wondered.

"It is complex. If I had time to explain, I would. We do not have three months for it, so the quick version is you, as Princess, will assume a position of opposition to political Russia. You will restore the Russian soul," Azrael stated. "Small children will want to be you. You will become a role model. All the small ones now have is Cheburashka. It is like Winnie the Pooh becoming a role model for American children. You can see the problem."

"I do not know this Winnie the Poop," Kat said.

Azrael laughed. "Your life will be difficult. But it has been difficult since age thirteen. You are also clever. Difficult is a concept you will eventually own. In the meantime, you will have the power to return to the Russian people their hearts."

"And I would have Faya and Sasha with me?" Kat asked.

"Your choice."

"You can tell me the worst and I will still make deal," Kat affirmed.

"I know you would. But that's you. So, deal?" Azrael asked.

"No question in my mind. It is deal." Katrinka considered. "When does this happen?"

"For Fay, the pain subsides beginning today. Her doctor will claim a miracle has occurred. All cancer gone," Azrael declared. "For you, it is a process, one of time. As they say, 'go with the flow.'"

"And you?" Kat asked.

"I will remain with Fay," Azrael answered. "One day the young woman, the kid from East LA, will reclaim her soul. It will be seamless."

"Can I add to the deal?" Kat inquired.

Azrael offered, "You can try me."

"When you decide to leave, will you tell me?" Kat asked.

"I will," Azrael agreed. "But I will be around. You can count on it. We have a lot of work ahead, you and

I."

"May I ask you, why me?" Kat wondered.

"I first noticed you when you killed Gabriel," replied Azrael.

Katrinka clutched her hands to her chest. "I killed an angel?" Kat gasped.

"An archangel, no less," Azrael confirmed.

A look of serious doubt claimed Kat's face. "That's worse."

"It may be," Azrael agreed. "You thought he was the man who would kill Irishka. Gabriel had taken his body when he died. The killing of an angel does not go unnoticed."

"I have big trouble for it?" Kat guessed.

"No. Gabriel moved on. It is not often a human kills one of God's chosen ones," Azrael told her. "So, like I said, it gets noticed. I then realized you possessed something special. I have a mission for you."

"The stones?" Kat speculated.

"Yes," Azrael replied. "The purpose of the stones will be known to you at a later time. In the meantime, guard them with your life."

"Of course."

"And from time to time, the two men you call topknots…" Azrael went on.

"Yes."

"They are who you surmised them to be. Angels," Azrael confirmed. "I don't want you to kill them. Okay?"

"I will try not to," Kat promised.

Azrael had finished her second bottle of beer. "Want another beer?" Kat offered.

"Sure. Why not?"

Katrinka retrieved yet another beer for Azrael. After she open it, she asked, "Do you want to watch TV?"

Chapter 10

A fair-skinned human sleeping in excess of two hours beside a swimming pool under the afternoon Parisian sun was a recipe for a serious sunburn. "Ma'am. Ma'am," were the words that interrupted Fay's nap. She opened her eyes.

"Ma'am," Azrael coaxed as she lightly jiggled Fay. "Wake up."

"Hey," Fay responded as she opened her eyes to survey her surroundings. "My God. How long have I been lying here?"

"Around two hours," Azrael informed her.

Fay surveyed her stomach and legs. "I should be burned to a crisp. I'm not."

"The pool staff told me you have been turning yourself," Azrael said. She previewed Fay's body. "You look okay to me. You may be a bit on the reddish side. Can I lotion you up?"

Fay sat up. She winched in pain and clutched her side.

"Are you okay, ma'am?" a concerned Azrael asked.

"Yes, yes. Fine." After taking a drink from her water bottle, Fay then laid on her front. "Go for it," she said. "What have you been up to all day? I hope it was fun."

Azrael squirted sun block onto the palms of her

hands. As she applied the lotion to Fay's back, she said, "I was shopping."

"Thanks for offering to lotion me up," Fay said. "Oh? Did you find anything interesting?"

"I did. I will claim it later."

The two women's conversation was cut short when Sasha approached.

"Sasha!" Fay greeted him. "Good afternoon. Are you having a pleasant day?"

"An outstanding day," he said. "How about you, Azrael?"

"A very good day," she replied.

Sasha said, "I have been cooped up in my room all day working. It occurred to me I should take a breath of fresh air."

"Did you have anything interesting in mind?" Fay inquired.

"Would you two ladies like to accompany me for an evening stroll around the Eiffel Tower and maybe a boat ride on the Seine?"

"I'm in!" Fay replied. "How about you, Azrael?"

Azrael offered, "The saying goes, 'two is company, three is a crowd.'"

Fay was disappointed.

Sasha said, "I like crowds. How about you, Faya?"

"I'm not about to visit the Tower without my people with me." She looked at Azrael. "Go get ready. And if I have to, I will make it an order. You are wasting time." Fay smiled. "Go!"

****

Three miles away

If a person was not paying attention when she stepped into a busy Parisian street, odds are, she may get hit by a car. Kat found herself on top of a table of surprised tourists who were enjoying something at one of the many Parisian sidewalk cafes. They were surprised, to say the least, but the pain she now felt in her left foot suggested she had broken bones. But she was lucky to be alive. Fortunately, the guys, who she knew as the topknots, assisted her off of the table...without trying to kill her. A taxi arrived seemingly out of nowhere. The helpful lads assisted her into the taxi and shut the door behind her, and the taxi sped off.

Katrinka tried to tell the driver, who spoke English, to drop her near the safehouse, but he would have none of it. "Hospital," he informed her.

In passing, she wondered about the topknots. They had had her right in the palms of their hands! And they had chosen to do nothing!

The French seemed to have a good health care system. Two hundred U.S. for X-rays, a walking cast, and three hours of her time, and Kat was good to go. Pretty normal stuff, really. But what she found odd was the driver who drove her to the hospital was the same guy who now drove her to the safehouse.

"How do you feel?" the apparently concerned driver asked.

"I am idiot," Katrinka replied.

The driver chuckled. "No. How is your foot?"

"Broken," Katrinka informed him. "I live."

"It could have been worse for you. A fast car, flying through the air, crash landing on a table?"

By now, Katrinka had grown suspicious of the driver. To test him, she asked in Russian, "Where is your family from?"

He replied in Russian, "Same as you. Russia."

Her suspicion was confirmed; he was a handler, probably Russian Military Service. Between the angels and the Russian Secret Service, no one was going to let her out of their sight. Well, there went her privacy!

The driver stopped within a block of the safehouse and wished her well. Knowing she was in need of snacks, beer and wine, and pain killers, Kat stopped at the local market. A sweet French boy noticed her struggle. He helped her with her shopping and then carried her grocery items to her home. Kat tipped the boy enough euros to likely equal his day's wages and limped inside.

After stowing her groceries, she opened a beer with her handy pocketknife and dropped onto the bed. She grabbed a pillow and, after placing it under her injured foot, she clicked on the TV. She had discovered she enjoyed old American films from the 1940s and 1950s. The costumes and hair styles were works of art. But she also wondered about a life, and the Americans seem particularly good at it, where one would go to work for an entire day, only to come home, sit in front of the TV, and then go to bed. And why in those movies did the husbands and wives sleep in separate beds? The next day, they repeated the same routine. What was that? She recalled her school lessons. Einstein had said it best, "Insanity is doing the same thing over and over and expecting different results." She hoped her life would never include this insanity.

Katrinka briefly considered placing a call to Fay to inform her about her foot. Then, she changed her mind. What could Fay do for her? Worry? Extreme exhaustion, stress, and the pain killers soon overcame her.

Gunfire awoke her. Instinctively, Kat reached for her 9MM. Quickly, she assured herself the chamber was loaded. The weapon was ready to fire. She listened. There was much loud talking. Then she heard a knock at the door. Katrinka rolled off of the bed opposite of the door, using the bed as a shield. Another knock came, this one sounding more urgent than the first.

A voice said, "We must go. Quickly."

Kat recognized the voice. She stood and limped to the door. With caution, she opened the door. It was who she thought it was: the taxi driver.

"Quickly. They have found you. You must hurry," he said.

Katrinka grabbed her backpack and stuffed her belongings into it. She retrieved the stones and her ID from the storage spot behind the framed picture. She followed the man from the room to his waiting taxi. At least two people lay on the sidewalk. They appeared dead. As the taxi sped away from the safehouse, Kat wondered who had shot whom and why.

The taxi sped along the busy street, the driver acting as if he were trying to lose a following car. She saw no evidence of this, but he seemed to know what he was doing. Then, the car stopped abruptly. He turned to her. He said something which sounded odd to her, "There are those who are threatened by *Novaya Rossiya*. Be careful, Princess Katrinka. We salute you." He added, "Get out."

Kat responded to his order. In an instant, another identical taxi screeched to a halt. This one had traveled in the direction from which they had just come. The rear passenger door opened.

"Get in," came a female voice from within the car.

Kat obeyed, and off the car sped. Soon, the taxi made an abrupt right turn. They were now flying down a very narrow alley. She estimated their speed to be in excess of 80 km/h. It was an insane speed but because the walls of the alley were so near to the car on either side, their speed seemed much faster. So, what would happen when this rocket ship got to the end of the alley? What about pedestrians and other cars, now unseen, traveling in the cross street? She recalled something Faya would often say: "Holy crap!" The meaning was somewhere lost in translation, yet it seemed to fit the moment.

****

The Eiffel Tower, across town

Fay stood on the first level deck, looking out over the city. The sun was setting in the west. She said to Sasha and Azrael, "It seems so peaceful."

"Should we go higher to the next level, ma'am?" Azrael asked.

"Let me get a selfie of us first." Fay produced her cell from her pocketbook. The three of them stood near the north rail with the Seine to their backs. Fay snapped three photos to ensure there was a good one for the photo log she had been creating of their time in Paris. After, she felt faint.

"Can we sit before we go up?" she asked. "I don't know what has come over me. I just need a moment to rest."

"Are you okay, ma'am?" Azrael was concerned.

"I'm okay," Fay lied. "Just a moment. I'm not ready to go." And she did not feel like her normal self this evening. She knew it was the cancer growing in her body. She wondered when the time would come for her to give up the fight and do as her doctor had recommended and submit to radiation treatment. Then the cat would be out of the bag. Everyone would know. Everyone would worry. And…well, she did not want to think about it. She also now sensed none of that would occur. Her time was now short.

As they sat, Azrael took her hand. Fay thought it strange Azrael would do that but she appreciated her gentleness just the same. For the moment, it was most comforting.

"Thank you, ma'am," Azrael said.

"For what, sweetheart?" Fay asked.

"For being you."

"I thought I was going to be sick there for a moment," Fay told her. "But now as I sit here with my friends and this beautiful view of this romantic city, I'm beginning to feel rejuvenated." Fay remained seated. She took in a refreshing breath of air and said, "I have to admit, for the first time, that I have not been well. I was told I have cancer."

Azrael listened.

Fay continued. "I don't know why but for some reason, I feel as if I am going to beat this sickness. I had given into defeat. But now, my attitude has changed, and I feel so very strong again."

Azrael listened as she continued to hold Fay's hand.

****

Near the end of the alley, Kat braced herself with stiffened arms, placing her hands on the back of the taxi's front seat. Instinctively closing her eyes, she held her breath. The car's four tires protested the abrupt right turn as the taxi accelerated along the Rue la Lafayette. Thank the gods, for the day all the French mothers and their babies strolling in the general vicinity of the alley were safe from harm. The driver must have been satisfied all was right with the world because she slowed the taxi's pace to a speed consistent with the accompanying traffic. The car came to a halt at a small hotel near the Metro Stalingrad Ligne 7 station.

How appropriate, Kat thought. *Typical of French to honor communist with street.*

The driver turned to her. Speaking in Russian, she said, "You live here. It will be safe." She added, "We live for *Novaya Rossiya.* Lady Katrinka. *Da svidaniya,*" she wished Kat.

Kat smiled, grabbed her backpack, and limped to the hotel's entrance. There was a reception desk near the entry. The woman was aware of Kat's arrival. She handed Kat a room key and pointed to Kat's assigned room on a map. The first-floor room was close in proximity to the front desk. Kat appreciated it because the location cut her limping distance considerably.

Kat found this room to be larger than her last room. The refrigerator and the TV were both larger as well. She quickly unpacked. She could not find a safe location to hide the stones. The backpack straps where she had first discovered the stones now became her hiding spots. Before she settled in for the night, she asked the reception attendant for a nearby café recommendation. The night attendant recommended La Chope and it was within limping distance. Also, the attendant gave her a crutch. Very nice. It made the limping almost bearable. La Chope offered takeout as well.

No one in France bothered to speak English. Hence, the all-French menu at Bistro La Chope presented a challenge. Some recognizable offerings were "burgers" and "beer." A young man seemed sympathetic. He did speak English and was willing to help translate the menu. Kat opted for the burger and beer anyway.

Back at her room, she settled in. The burger and beer were the first food she had had for the day. The French had a different concept of what a burger was, but a beer was always a beer. Kat decided if she were to eat another hamburger in France, it would be an American one. Earlier, she had learned restaurant food was more expensive in Paris. No one bothered to mention they all included a tip in the price, leaving the unsuspecting diner to pay a second tip for any meal, including fast food. The day one discovered this double tipping dipping became one of those "ah ha" moments.

Following dinner, Kat utilized a plastic shower bag the hospital staff had given her to keep her foot dry. Following the refreshing shower, sleep was next on her agenda. She sent a quick text to Faya to assure her she was safe and sound.

Kat was awakened early the follow morning by the pain associated with the broken bone in her foot. A few pain killers were all it took to get her day started off on the right foot. Her day would begin with breakfast. One of the few things she appreciated about the French, and maybe it was the Russian in her, was their simple approach to the first meal of the day. Bread, which was necessary for the consumption of the main course, jam. Add coffee, or tea, and juice. Unlike Americans, Northern Europeans, and Russians, Kat wondered why the French had a need for chickens and pigs in their morning diet.

The crutch the people at the hotel had given her was working out well, both as a walking aide but also, in a pinch, a useful weapon.

It seemed no sooner had she made her deal with Azrael, people began trying to run her over with a car and shots were fire outside her safehouse. A safehouse! The news traveled fast. Could it be the good angels and the bad angels had begun a war? Over her? There were only a few times in her life where Kat had felt vulnerable, like what a deer in hunting season must feel or like a little fox being chased around by people with dogs and guns. It seemed like a reprise of spy school where some crazy was continually jumping out from somewhere to test her defensive and reaction skills. Hell, they would even wait until she was in the lav and then they would come at her from over the top of the stall. Catch her with her pants down, so to speak. Her reflexes were so well conditioned if anyone were to come at her from behind with so much as a friendly tap on the shoulder, her reflexes would lay them low. Fay had learned early on to let Kat know she was somewhere in the vicinity at all times.

While Kat ate her breakfast, she recollected her recent past, which began with her discovery she was heir to the nonpolitical leadership of Russia, plus the title of Princess and 90 million U.S. dollars. She had been thrown in a Cairo prison, only to have the angel of death facilitate her escape. Then came the train ride across Europe, where she had discovered a fortune in conflict diamonds hidden in her borrowed backpack. Next was the foiled bombing of the French Embassy in

Budapest. And within the past two days someone had tried to run her over and there had been gun play outside of her safe home. And then she had received the sad news her Faya was dying of cancer. No, she did not want to be the next Princess of Russia, but it was her only option. It was what she had agreed to in her bargain with an angel.

Spy school classes related to heath care had taught her how to manage pain and injury while still focusing on the mission at hand. As a result, Kat was adept at minor body repair while on the fly. She had experienced muscle sprains in the past but never a broken bone. The objective with a break was to accelerate the healing, thus shortening the downtime. After breakfast, she made her way to a nearby *Pharmacie 217*. Her training recommended antioxidants, protein-rich mineral supplements, and vitamin supplements. A diet of fish, beef, and beer, plus exercise, were also on her list.

Kat next inserted the cell battery into her phone and sent a text to Azrael: *I fight with car. Car won. Foot broken. I am okay. Went to hospital. Now relocated.*

Azrael messaged back: *You will be okay. You're the badass. Remember? We have your back.*

Kat responded: *More like a dumbass. Take care.*

She clicked off the phone. She would leave it to Azrael to tell Faya or not. The rest of her day was TV and rest.

Chapter 11

Sofitel Paris Baltimore Tour Eiffel Hotel

Fay lay on her room's balcony sunbed, thinking about life. Soon she, Azrael, and Sasha planned to tour the Notre-Dame de Paris or "Our Lady of Paris." Our Lady had been fully restored after suffering a devastating fire several years prior. The plan was to meet in the hotel lobby in about an hour.

There came a knock at her door. She thought it might be room service or a room attendant. The voice accompanying the knock proved it to be Azrael.

"Just a moment!" Fay said as she rose from the sunbed and proceeded to the door.

Fay greeted Azrael at the door. "Hi, Azrael. You look great!"

"Hi, ma'am," Azrael replied. "You look great, too. I was in the hotel fitness center for my daily workout routine. How do you feel today?"

"You know, funny you should ask," she said. "I was just now laying on the balcony and the Tower is so captivating I tried but couldn't find an ache or pain I usually contend with." Fay's eyes brightened. "So, I guess I am having a good day! Are we still on for Notre-Dame?"

"Yes, we are. I have a feeling when you finally return home, you are going to learn from your doctor you are winning this one," Azrael encouraged her. "Just like you always do, ma'am."

Fay laughed. "The jury is still out, I am afraid."

Azrael offered a knowing smile. "While I was lifting," she said, "I got a message from Lady K. I wanted to share it with you right away."

"Of course!" Fay was excited. "Come. Let's sit on the balcony."

After they had made themselves comfortable on the two sunbeds, Azrael said, "Like I said, I got a text from Katrinka."

"I received one from her last night as well," Fay added.

"Good news and bad news, ma'am," Azrael cautioned. "So, sit tight."

A look of concern grew on Fay's face.

"First she and a car had an incident." Before Fay could respond, Azrael added, "She is okay. She has a broken foot. Has been to a hospital. They told her the foot will be as good as new in six to twelve weeks."

"Just her foot?" Fay asked with concern. "Otherwise, she is okay?"

"Ma'am, remember we are talking about Lady K," Azrael reminded Fay. "She has been doing this kind of stuff since she was, like, thirteen years old."

"Well, true. But still I need to be concerned." Fay smiled. "Did she say anything else?"

"She moved to a new location," Azrael relayed. "Her life is growing more complicated. Good news is, Irishka will be with her. In the meantime, why not text her? Maybe she can meet you?"

Fay said, "I am absolutely thrilled you and Katrinka are forming a bond. I had hoped for the longest time she would find a meaningful girlfriend relationship. We gals sometimes need the outlets to share problems, feelings, thoughts, and successes we get from those close girlfriend bonds. I know she has Irishka as a role model but it's not the same as a girlfriend bond."

Azrael confirmed, "Lady K is a most unique woman. I would love to be her friend."

Fay's phone chimed. She clicked on the phone. "Fay," she answered. A wide smile formed on her lips. "For sure. Where? When? Okay, I will tell him." She clicked off the phone.

"Lady K?" Azrael guessed.

"Yes, she will meet us tomorrow. Sasha will have the details."

****

Rue la Lafayette, a safehouse, Paris, France.

It was 10:00 A.M. when Katrinka heard the knock at her door. She was expecting Fay, Sasha, and Azrael. Sasha would have ensured they had not been followed from the hotel to her room.

She had prepared tea, coffee, bread and jam for her guests. With pent-up excitement in her heart, she hopped on her broken foot to the door. Upon opening the door, there was a rush of hugs and kisses all around. The joy emanated was over the top.

Katrinka offered everyone a seat. She only had two. Azrael and Sasha chose the only chairs in the room, while Katrinka laid on the bed with Fay beside her at her feet.

After Fay had elevated her foot for her, Katrinka said, "I am so happy we are all here." She looked at Sasha with a smile on her lips and love in her eyes.

"How are you, Papa?"

Sasha returned the smile. "I am better than everyone," he said.

"Faya and Azrael, I am so happy now. Can I offer tea, coffee, and bread?" Kat asked.

All accepted her offer and Fay served their requests.

"Well," Katrinka began, "Irishka would be here, but she is nearby watching." Katrinka explained, "She has room down hall." She took a breath. "I have decision made. I will return to Russia, but I must explain my decision."

Fay offered, "We will support whatever your decision is, Katrinka."

Katrinka again smiled. "I owe explanation. It is important for me." Katrinka looked at Fay. "Faya," she said, "you have given me my life. I will never forget and will always appreciate you for giving me a home and taking me as your adopted daughter. And I will soon realize one of my dreams to become American citizen."

A tear ran from Fay's right eye. She wiped it away with the back of her right hand.

"Papa, you and Irishka," Kat continued, "took me from life of Sparrow and gave me pride and purpose as agent for Russian military. For it, I am forever grateful."

Sasha also had a tear or two to offer.

Kat next looked at Azrael. "So much to tell about my angel," she said.

Azrael nodded, a nod signaling her permission for Katrinka to tell all about their relationship.

Katrinka smiled. "Faya and Sasha," she went on,

"you will believe me when I tell you what I am about to tell you. You have both accepted time travel as a fact because we have all lived it. Now, I want you to know about Azrael."

Azrael once again offered her a nod of encouragement.

"Where do I start?" Kat mused. "I met Azrael at prison in Cairo. She helps me to escape."

Fay offered Azrael an appreciative smile.

"You see, Azrael is Azrael. You know her as Angel of Death," Kat revealed. "*Angel Smerti*, Papa."

Sasha's eyes widened. He offered a knowing nod.

"She had come to be with Faya, Papa." Katrinka looked at Fay. "Faya," she said, "you die from the cancer. You tell no one, but how do I know it? Angel explain me she would help you on trip to afterlife. But something happened. She spent time with you and learned Faya has good and kind soul. So, she say to me would I consider deal? My soul for Faya soul? I agreed, yes, immediately."

"No!" Fay exclaimed. "I cannot allow it. No."

Katrinka said, "Wait. I will tell more. Deal is done. Then we talk about it, and I agree to make compromise."

Fay appeared dejected. Her voice was weak as she repeated, "No."

"Fay," Azrael said, "Listen to her."

Fay nodded, yes.

"So, we make deal." Kat resumed speaking. "Angel will trade Faya's soul if I agree to accept headship of Russia as Princess Yekaterina Romanova-Lavrova. I think it is best deal. I hope you all think so."

Sasha, as a Russian close to the political construct

of his country, saw the logic in Katrinka's decision. He offered to Fay, "It is for best, Faya. I am happy for her, and she has my undying support."

With gratitude, Katrinka offered, "Thank you, Papa. I have told Irishka of my choice. She agree with me."

Sasha said to Fay, "As headship, she can do much for the people of Russia, but also for the people of the world. Remember Princess Diana Spencer?"

Fay nodded.

Sasha continued, "Lady Di had no political power, yet she had charisma. Her heart touched everyone in the world. You know it as true. This is what is possible for Katrinka. But this is bigger deal." With kindness in his eyes, he reminded Fay, "When you first met me, it was aboard U.S.S. *Green*. Do you remember it?"

Fay nodded again.

"I said there was a time when I could feel the soul of the Russian people in the streets of Moscow," Sasha reminded her. "It was a time when the air was filled with softness and tenderness. Now, I feel sadness in my heart for the old mother-country, for a once glorious *Rossiya*…and for her proud and distant past. Now, my friend, as you well know, *Moskva* has become Western in its ways. But the soul…the soul now remains buried deep within her." Sasha smiled. "Katrinka may be our hope."

"Faya," Katrinka added, "you say you feel better like never before. Azrael say the cancer is leaving your body. You will live long happy life. Is okay?"

"I don't know what to say," Fay replied. She looked at Azrael. "Thank you. I am forever in your debt."

Azrael emphasized, "I do not know the future, nor can I predict it. With your love and support, Lady K can do anything."

"I will do everything in my power," Fay pledged.

Azrael spoke to Katrinka. "You remind me, Lady K, of a girl I once knew." Azrael recalled, "She was Boudicca and they called her 'Warrior Queen.' This was around the first century AD. Her tribe was the British Iceni. The Romans pissed her off, so with good reason, she formed a posse, went to London, proceeded to burn it to the ground, and wiped out about eighty thousand Roman soldiers along the way."

"I could not do it," Katrinka protested.

"No, certainly not," Azrael assured her. "But you have the clever strength of a Boudicca. Or even Jeanne d'Arc, one of my favorites. Forty thousand statues cannot be wrong. And I always tell you, Lady K, you are a badass. And I knew many, so I know a badass when I see one. You just harness it in a different and more productive way. I will say again, I cannot see the future, nor do I even try to predict the future," Azrael explained. "I can see the potential for the future. I know you are reluctant, Lady K, and you have made it clear you do not want this. I believe you can do this, and you can do it well, for the betterment of all the Russian people. You cannot do it alone, and no one expects you to. You have good support. Your people are strong. Never underestimate their powers of love, trust, and loyalty."

Katrinka diverted her eyes away from Azrael. She then refocused them on the angel. With renewed hope and determination in her voice, she vowed, "With help, I can do it."

****

Fay and Sasha must have finished their discussion about the diamonds. Fay asked Katrinka, "Kat, Sasha and I were talking about the diamonds. Sasha has a safe in his room at the hotel. Would you be comfortable letting him store them in his safe?"

Sasha added, "We think the stress the diamonds may be causing you would be relieved if you did not have to think about them. At least until your foot heals."

Katrinka glanced at Azrael. Azrael nodded her approval.

"Okay. Thank you, papa," Kat said, scooping the stones worth an estimated twenty million dollars, and change, back into the two bags. When done, she looked at the two bags and commented, "One stone is missing?"

Azrael laughed and tossed the stone to her.

Katrinka snatched the stone from the air, also laughing. "You test me," she said.

Fay commented she felt more at ease with the diamonds now in Sasha's care. Yet, her worry for her daughter's safety and health were still foremost on her mind. "It must be my maternal instincts on high alert? I feel like I have somehow failed," she confessed to the group.

"Ma'am," Azrael offered, "I have known many mothers in my time. You are allowed to feel the way you do. These feelings will serve to allow you to grow stronger."

Fay smiled. "Thank you."

Azrael added, "Yes, Katrinka's decision to assume the headship, although a reluctant one, places her in harm's way. There are some who would like to control her power, as did Lenin with Russia."

"It seems our political systems have historically been in upheaval for a thousand years," Sasha said. "Many will initially see this as a threat to our current political system. Others will hope it to be that which it is, an opportunity to restore the heart and soul of the old Russia."

"I now understand why Katrinka's uncle, Prince Eugen, bowed out. And I do understand Katrinka's reluctance to tackle this head on," Fay said to Azrael. "We are all here, including Irishka, for Kat. And if my hunch is correct, I believe, if given a choice, the Marine Guard I first met at the U.S. Embassy in Cairo will want to be involved as well. I am really impressed with Corporal Lopez."

Azrael added, "I will always be somewhere, Lady K, if for no other reason than to keep track of Mazikim. We do not want another Rasputin to cloud the scene."

"Mazikim?" Katrinka questioned.

"Dear, sweet Mazikim. She sits at Lucifer's right hand as his punisher," Azrael explained. "Rasputin was a natural for her. He was the guy who invented bad personal hygiene. Literally, he smelled like hell. He was divisive and repulsive. His influence discredited your ancestors, the Romanov family, and may have led to their eventual demise."

Fay informed them, "I am being pressed by the JAG because my extended leave of absence ends soon. My boss has an assignment open on a carrier now stationed in the South China Sea. He said the U.S. is undergoing a military buildup there."

Sasha replied, "I as well. Russian Navy asks for my

return, and I would think Irishka may have been contacted as well."

"So, it would seem we are at a crossing point in Lady K's life," Azrael surmised.

Sasha suggested, "I should text Irishka to join us?"

All agreed to his proposal. While Sasha worked at constructing the message and then sending it, the others continued to plan.

Sasha reported, "Irishka is now in hall. She will be here momentarily."

Shortly, there came a knock at the door. Azrael leapt up in response to the knock.

Irishka entered the room and smiled at everyone. "What's up?" she asked in a cheerful tone.

Sasha told her, "We are discussing what our next move will be. You know Katrinka has agreed to return to Moscow to begin plans to assume headship of Romanov family?"

Irishka nodded in agreement. "I go where Yekaterina goes. No question." She surveyed the room. "Room is crowded for meeting. There is private courtyard behind hotel."

Sasha suggested, "Shall we move? Katrinka, how do you feel like walking?"

Katrinka confirmed. "Is no problem for me. Let's go."

Chapter 12

The courtyard was artistically landscaped with pots of live flowers and small trees. The white walls intensified the sun's natural light. The courtyard provided the warm seclusion needed for their privacy. Fay placed a chair facing the chair Katrinka sat in, allowing the other woman to elevate her broken foot.

Katrinka admired her broken foot, with toes exposed, and observed, "At least I can paint my toes. I am getting idea what it is to be princess," she mused.

Azrael laughed. "You, Lady K, were a princess on the day of your birth. You just did not know it."

Fay had stopped by the hotel reception to order room service to be delivered to the courtyard: coffee, tea, soft drinks, and sandwiches. She so informed those in attendance.

Katrinka adjusted the pillow placed under her broken leg and began the discussion. "Thank you, my family. I cannot make these choices without your opinions and advices."

"All of us are here for you," Fay assured her. "We will always be."

Katrinka smiled. "I have question and a few concerns. One of big ones is how do I travel to Moscow? I think it possible both Interpol...come to think of it, Apple Cheeks found me while I was traveling from Cairo to Paris."

"Apple Cheeks?" Irishka queried.

Katrinka puffed her cheeks in response to Irishka's apparent memory loss.

This drew a chuckle from Irishka, who normally did not chuckle. "Popov," she replied.

"Oh, yes," Kat confirmed. "That *klaun*."

"Oh," Fay said, "that guy. Yes, I have met the chap several times."

Katrinka continued. "And Egyptian police want me for escape from Cairo prison? And maybe someone died too."

Azrael smiled. "Odd," she lamented.

Sasha started, "I have been considering it…"

This did not surprise Fay in the least. Her pal Lavrov was a genius, in her opinion.

"I do not think you can travel from civilian airport or rail station without your travel being noticed." Sasha added, "We will have Russian government plane, or train, transport Katrinka, Irishka and me from Paris to Moscow. Result is no customs necessary."

"That is brilliant, Sasha," Fay complimented him.

"Question two," Katrinka asked. "When I arrive at Moscow, what next?"

Sasha had plan number two ready to share. "Until we know further, and for your protection, I have spoken to President Rudkovsky's security chief about this. He told me you will live at Kremlin in special military housing. After your foot heals, then we make next move. In meantime, you will meet with President Rudkovsky and staff for bonding." Sasha turned to Fay. "Faya, your thoughts?" he prompted.

Fay was beaming. She was reunited with her daughter. Everything else was a bonus as far as she was concerned. "I am good with the plan," she responded. "I only want what is best for Katrinka."

Azrael answered Fay with logic and reason, "Ma'am, the mother in you will always want and hope for the best for your daughter. Let her have her wings. I know, I know, it's a saying. But you know what I mean."

The Angel of Death looked into Fay's eyes, expressing more compassion through her own eyes than few mortals had ever experienced. Fay felt a deep, loving warmth course through her soul.

Then Azrael asked Fay, "Did Jeanne d'Arc's mother worry? Probably. Did Lady Di's mother worry? Probably. And I could go on and on with thousands of years of examples of mothers caring about their daughters." Azrael smiled. "Trust in me. Lady K has survived extraordinary odds to be here with us today. Going on, her strength to survive will continue to serve her well."

Fay straightened her back and slapped her knees with her hands. "Okay, you had me at 'trust.'"

Katrinka added, "You had me too. I feel so much better about this." With a renewed look of determination on her face, she declared, "I will do it!"

A broad smile crossed the angel's face. "Lady K...Yekaterina, I cannot wait for the world to meet you."

Katrinka nodded her head and whispered an appreciative, "Thank you." Now, with heartfelt concern, she asked Fay, "Faya, what about Binky?"

Fay chuckled. "I wondered when you would get around to Binky." Fay explained to the others, "Binky is Katrinka's cat, the one she had always wanted from childhood." Fay directed her answer to Katrinka. "Binky is now living with JP on her farm. You knew that. I understand she is a great mouse catcher. She has a great temporary home, and my sister and her husband love her. They will send Binky to you wherever and whenever you choose." Fay thought for a moment and then added, "Did JP text you a video?"

A fond memory brought a smile to Kat's lips. "My phone is the crap." Katrinka showed Fay her cheap cell phone. "I may have video?" She shrugged her shoulders.

"Here," Fay responded as she retrieved her cell from her pocketbook, "I have a photo of Binky."

Katrinka seemed amused as she studied the photo of her beloved cat. She then offered the phone to Azrael, Sasha, and Irishka. Geez. Okay. Time to move on.

Katrinka recapped the plan, as she understood it. "Papa and Irishka will come with me to Moscow. Faya will return to Navy and maybe ship in South China Sea." She next looked at Azrael. "What about you, dear angel?"

Azrael wondered aloud, "I do not know about me. I enjoy being human. It has been a good holiday for me. Yet, I have more to do before I leave." She looked at Fay with hope in her eyes.

Fay understood her silent question. "Sweetheart, if I am on my way to the South China Sea, I will need my staff. Petty Officer Winslow is a single man. He will be given a choice, of course, but my intuition tells me he will be thrilled to serve on a United States aircraft carrier," Fay informed Azrael. "As for my sister, JP, I would not ask her. She would naturally honor my request. Yet, if she did, then she may be committing to being a long time away from her husband and, because he is a Navy sea captain, he is already away from home as it is. As a result, I have an opening."

Azrael, with a look of hope on her face, asked, "Can I apply for the open spot, ma'am?"

Fay laughed. "I thought you would never ask!" Fay rose from her chair, took a few short steps toward Azrael, and hugged her. "We will request a transfer from the Embassy Security detail to JAG Corp. You just say the word and I will make it happen."

Azrael continued to embrace Fay. The angel was crying.

Fay observed, "Do I see angel tears?"

Azrael nodded and sniffed. "Yes, ma'am."

Irishka snatched a tissue from a nearby table and handed it to Azrael.

Azrael said, "In all of my years, I have not experienced an aircraft carrier." She was serious when she next asked Fay an odd question, "Do you think someone would let me fly in a fighter jet?"

Fay replied to her mystifying question, "You have wings? Why?"

"It is a part of my human experience, ma'am." Azrael laughed as she rose from her chair. There was a whoosh sound as her magnificent silver-gray angel wings appeared on her shoulders, creating enough turbulence in their unfolding that several of the drink cups spilled. All were awed to witness a sight few humans had ever experienced.

****

One week later, JAG HQ, Bremerton, Washington
Fay, Petty Officer Winslow, Petty Officer Fletcher,

and Corporal Lopez met in Fay's office to discuss their game plan for the next two weeks.

Fay directed the conversation. "Azrael, we discussed you are going home to LA to see your family. You have ten days leave, then you will be back here for our departure planning. In the meantime, Don, JP, and I are going to provide legal support for the JAG." Fay instructed Don Winslow, "Don, we are assigned to the U.S.S. *Ronald Reagan*. Do you know where she is now?"

Don used his tablet to locate the *Reagan's* current whereabouts. "Near north of Manila, ma'am."

"Okay," Fay said. "We have had good luck with Delta Air Lines in the past. Don, see if the Navy will book three one-way." Fay added an additional request, "Ask the Navy logistics officer if we can fly business class. I will pay the up-charge."

He began typing on his tablet. "The date of travel, ma'am?" Winslow asked.

"Not knowing how we are going to travel from Manila to the *Reagan*, why not give us an extra day in Seoul and I can contact Colonel Jangho Kim. Maybe for dinner?" Fay appeared somewhat dejected when she said, "I want to minimize our travel from land to the *Reagan* by chopper to the fewest possible hours."

Azrael wrinkled her brow. "Don't like choppers, ma'am?" she asked.

"You got it, sister," Fay informed her. "Noisy, cold, uncomfortable, no real place to…Well, you get my point."

"You know," Azrael observed, "that's what I told Leonardo."

"DiCaprio?" Winslow asked, not aware he was in

the presence of one of God's big dogs, a ten-gazillion-year-old archangel who had most likely consulted or advised Da Vinci on a number of occasions, including his design of the "airscrew." Winslow looked it up once informed they were referring to the other Leonardo. Yet, he still unsure of the meaning of Azrael's comment.

Fay could only laugh and shake her head. She had a mission for JP as well. "Sis, I know you must be disappointed, and if you want, I can still wiggle you a spot on this carrier assignment. But do you want to be at sea for six months and spend that much time away from your new hubby?" Fay asked.

There was enough collective doubt evident in JP's expression for Fay to add, "Let me know soon what you want, and I will make it happen." Fay gave her sister a reassuring smile. "In the meantime, will you call or text Katrinka and let her know how her Binky is? She did not get the video you sent her. And although I did share another text with her, she has been worried about her kitty. So maybe an update?"

JP said, "You got it, ma'am." She added, "Binky is great at catching mice. She will spend the entire day in the barn. Why, I think the barn is now mouse-free." JP sighed. "Problem is, she brings them to the house!"

Everyone had a good laugh at that one.

Fay said to Azrael, "Are you ready to get yourself off to LA?"

"This evening, I think," Azrael replied.

JP and Winslow seemed somewhat lost during the conversation between Fay and Azrael, but they both wished her a pleasant journey.

****

That evening at Fay's home, Bremerton, Washington

Fay and Azrael were talking in Fay's kitchen while Fay prepared spaghetti for the two women.

Azrael tapped on the small aquarium on Fay's kitchen counter. "What are your fishes' names?"

"Joey and Garfield," Fay replied. "The guppy is Joey. I named him after my friend Chicago mob boss Joey 'The Guppy' Stumpanato."

Azrael laughed. "Cute!" she affectionally replied. She added, "After dinner, I will lay on the sofa to watch TV. I am going to fall asleep. Later, Corporal Lopez will wake back up. You are going to have to be ready to help her. This is hard for humans. She will be very disoriented and frightened."

Fay wrinkled her brow, concerned. "How can I help her?"

"She will recognize you. So, that will help her," Azrael assured Fay.

"What next?"

"Have a shot of whiskey ready."

"Whiskey?" Fay was confused.

"Trust me," Azrael assured Fay. "The whiskey will help calm her."

"Geez!" Fay exclaimed. "This is a big deal!"

"Yeah," Azrael said, "it is huge." She then smiled. "No, I'm just kidding with you. Not to worry, you will figure it out."

"Thanks, I think?" Fay added, "Is this the last we will see of you?"

"Yes," Azrael said. She thought for a moment. "I may come back. But I will first warn you." Azrael informed her. "Deal?"

"I will hold you to it," Fay insisted. She then held the Angel of Death tight. "Thank you for all you have done. And thank you for my life." Fay reconsidered. Using her fingers, she counted, "The Arizona desert, the warehouse in Seattle, the ship in Korea... and? Oh, and the alligator, and the shark, and the cancer."

"Yeah, you gave me the slip every time. But I will get you yet, girlfriend," Azrael teased. Azrael then responded by giving Fay a kiss on her cheek. "The pleasure has been all mine." Lady Death then whispered, "Tell you what. When your time comes, I promise it will be I who accompanies you to the afterlife. It is the least I can do. Besides, for the longest time I have been looking for a good helper. Good help is hard to find these days."

Fay must have had a look of doubt on her face.

"Okay," Azrael reassured Fay, "how about an administrative assistant?"

"Better!" Fay said cheerfully. "I'm in! And you promise me I get first shot at the job?"

Azrael nodded her head, yes. She then glanced at the stove. "Better tend to the spaghetti before it boils over." She then glanced at the aquarium again. "This Guppy fellow. Is he someone I should know?"

Fay emitted a short laugh. "Ah, leave him alone. He's a nice guy. Just misguided. You know, when I was in the hospital for weeks and weeks, that guy and his mob lawyer sent me a flower arrangement every day! Imagine that!"

"Sweet," Azrael replied. "I suppose he will find his way to me soon enough."

Following dinner, Azrael asked Fay one more time if she was ready to get Marine Corporal Azrael Lopez rebooted. She did offer, "If you don't want to go through this, we can get Lopez to the hospital. When she opens her eyes, you can tell her she got knocked on the head in Cairo and she had amnesia. That's the normal way we do it."

Fay did not hesitate. "No. I want to be honest with her," she insisted.

Azrael said, "That is what I like about you, Faydra. You're a pure-heart." She hugged Fay again. "Ready to go?"

Fay nodded. Fay and Azrael proceeded to the living room sofa. Azrael reclined, resting with her head on a pillow.

Fay asked, "Before you go, do you mind if I ask you something?"

"Was it your time when we were on the Tower?" Azrael guessed.

Fay nodded.

"You knew it was your time. You remember I asked you if you were ready to go to the next level?"

Fay again nodded, yes.

"When I met you sunning beside the pool in Cairo, I had told you I had been shopping, but I had really just come from meeting with Lady K," Azrael disclosed. "We had reached an agreement where, in exchange for your soul, she would accept the headship of the Romanov family."

Fay bit her lower lip. Tears welled in her eyes, but she remained silent.

Azrael continued speaking. "You know Lady K agreed and I still think it is best for all. Anyway, while I rubbed the lotion on your back, I was surprised to learn your sickness was much more advanced than I had realized. Your time had come. But Sasha came and asked us to join him for a tour of the Tower. You wanted to decline. You were very sick and wanted to go to your room, where you would have died that night in your sleep," Azrael revealed. "Because you are who you are, you did not want to disappoint your friend, so you fought through it. Your determination and devotion to your friends touched me deeply. So, by the time we got to the Tower, you were done. I asked if you were ready to go to the next level. Most would have said yes. But you fought me, as you had many times before. You knew in your heart what I meant because you then knew who I really was. Your commitment to continue the fight, even though you knew it was a losing battle, was the confirmation I needed from you to take the sickness, rather than you."

"Thank you, "Fay said. "I very much look forward to our next meeting."

Before she closed her eyes, the Angel of Death smiled, winked, and said, "See ya around, kiddo." She closed her eyes.

It seemed to Fay as if a very dear friend had died. She rose from the sofa, walked across the room, retrieved the remote, and clicked on the TV. She returned to the sofa, covered her friend with a soft blanket, then sat to await Azrael's reawakening.

Chapter 13

Vélizy – Villacoublay Air Base, France

Sasha, Irishka, and Katrinka waited in a chilled mild breeze outside of the air base's passenger station as the Russian government *Sukhoi Superjet* 100 taxied toward them. Finally, the jet came to a stop and shut its twin engines down.

Speaking in Russian, Katrinka remarked to Sasha, "It's a big airplane, papa. Just for us?"

Sasha smiled as they all walked toward the Russian jet. "It is special transportation of important government people, Yekaterina."

As they neared the aircraft, the left forward passenger door popped open. Two husky Russian military men hustled down the stairway and quickly made their way to a limping Katrinka, who was supported on either side by Irishka and Sasha. Both were struggling to assist Katrinka while managing all of their assorted luggage. When the men arrived at her side, Kat draped her arms over their broad shoulders. The men walked back toward the jet, almost lifting her from the ground in doing so.

Katrinka was tall, but light for the two big men as they carried her up the passenger stairs and into the cabin of the jet. As she made her way to a nearby seat, she noticed the ultra-plush passenger accommodations.

"It is like first class," she commented to Irishka.

"What is government plane," Irishka said in a sarcastic tone of voice.

The three passengers buckled in. The jet's engines wound back up and, within a few minutes, the aircraft rolled forward and made its way to the runway. The jet paused while the pilots waited for two French fighter jets to take off. The plane again moved forward, turning from the tarmac onto the runway. Without delay, the jet accelerated forward and lifted off into the early morning sky.

Once airborne, several flight attendants came by asking for food and drink orders. To Katrinka, they all seemed somewhat shy.

Sasha noticed their behavior as well. "The attendants seem to know who you are. This begins the royal treatment, I believe, princess," he surmised.

During the flight, the four cabin attendants seemed to want to chat with Kat. And she accommodated them. Katrinka realized the attendants had not met a real princess before. After all, she did not yet consider herself any more significant than she did when she was that thirteen-year-old *femme fatale* in training from years gone by. Truth be known, Katrinka had not met a bona fide princess either. It was her future job to make herself the people's princess.

Following the meal service, one of the cabin attendants, who Katrinka assumed to be the bravest of the crew, came to her and softly and most politely asked Katrinka if she might bother her for her autograph. Katrinka gladly obliged. Katrinka was quickly getting the hang of this princess business. She asked the attendant, a woman of her approximate age, if she wanted to include a selfie. The attendant was quick to produce a cell phone. Several nice photos ensued. This seemed to open the flood gates. Shortly afterward, three other polite flight attendants approached Katrinka with the same requests. Next came group photos. In the end, Katrinka found herself in the cockpit sitting in the copilot's seat with his hat on and several more selfies of the pilots and her posing as if she were in command of the aircraft. She later told Sasha she thoroughly enjoyed every moment of the attention she was getting.

"You well know, Yekaterina, I told you one day you would be *yelikaya knyaginya*," Sasha stated.

"You told me many things, papa," Katrinka softly reminded him. "You and Irishka are my family. You know, papa, you may not recall many of those things you say to me." She patted his hand. "But I remember every single word."

****

Six hours had passed since Azrael had fallen asleep. The angel had failed to tell Fay how long Azrael would sleep. Fay awoke to find the morning sun's rays had managed to find their way through her drawn curtains. All-night TV-watching tended to eventually put one to sleep. Overdosing on back-to-back Bogie and Bacall black and whites left something to be desired. *Now, they had a great love story, but what was that Warren Beatty/Natalie Wood flick*, Fay wondered? *Splendor in the something or other?* Repressed love and sexual frustrations. She did not need them to remind her.

The TV was still on, now featuring one of the cheery good morning shows. Lots of women yacking about something she could care less about. Fay had to chuckle. Sometime during the night, a pillow had found its way onto Fay's lap, along with Azrael's sweet head. And sometime during the night, her boredom must have inspired her to braid Azrael's hair. Fay grabbed her cell. Selfies would be required. Fay did not know too many people who slept with a full-blown smile etched onto their face.

Azrael stirred. Her eyes popped open; she hesitated, then quickly rose from her slumber. "What the hell?" were the first words out of her mouth. She first looked at Fay with a measure of what seemed to be a combination of panic and confusion.

Rightly so, Fay thought.

"Good morning, Azrael," Fay greeted her.

Azrael rechecked her surroundings. She discovered her braids and said, with a braid in each hand, "Ma'am? What the...?"

Fay reassured her, "We are okay. Take a few breaths and I will explain."

The Marine in Azrael obeyed and sat back and yawned. After a stretch, she asked, "Where am I?"

Fay answered, "You are in my home."

As expected, Azrael was disoriented and confused. "Ma'am, I was in a cab with that lawyer guy in Cairo. I blacked out, I think? Now we are here?" She again reconfirmed her surroundings. "Where are we?"

"My home. In Bremerton. Near the navy yard," Fay explained.

Once satisfied her geography related questions were now answered, Azrael next went to that which was most important. "Ma'am, I am hungry," she informed Fay. "And, like, I am really dehydrated. And I have to pee."

"Okay," Fay acknowledged, "that's a lot to deal with all at once." Fay pointed toward her bathroom. "That way," she directed.

Azrael nodded her head and said, "Thank you, ma'am." She hesitated. "It still is 'ma'am,' isn't it?"

Fay affirmed with a slight nod. She pointed again. "Go! I will get you a glass of milk and a bite of something to eat."

Azrael nodded.

By the time Fay had returned with the milk and a bowl of Wheaties, Azrael was patiently waiting for her.

"You have a really nice home, ma'am," Azrael stated. "I like your bathroom."

"Thank you, dear." Fay knew she had forgotten something. "Go ahead and start. I'll get orange juice."

As Fay moved toward the kitchen, Azrael asked, "Can I have a cola too, ma'am?"

Fay remarked, "You really are thirsty!"

"I really am. Like someone left me out in the Sahara Desert for a week without water."

Fay returned to sit with Azrael while she consumed her cereal, juice, milk… and then asked for seconds.

When Fay thought Azrael was finally settled, she poured a shot of whiskey for each of them, as the angel had instructed. She handed the whiskey to Azrael and said, "Drink this and then I am going to explain to you why and how you are here."

Azrael eagerly nodded. She accepted the whiskey and without question or doubt, she gulped it down. "I am ready."

Fay clicked off the TV. Her cell chimed. She glanced at it to see if it was important. She adjusted the chime to vibrate and set the phone aside. Then, glancing at the phone, she asked Azrael, "Will you remind me later where I put my phone, should I ask?"

"Yes, ma'am."

"I'm counting on you, Corporal Lopez."

"Dang!' Azrael exclaimed. "I'm still a corporal?!"

"For the time being," Fay assured her. "You said your last memory was from the return trip after you met Katrinka at the prison," she prompted.

"Lady K," Azrael recalled. "How is she, ma'am? Is she still in prison? Or did we get her out?"

"Good news in that regard. Thanks to you, yes, she is out and now in Moscow."

"Thank, God," Azrael said as she crossed herself. In doing so, her hand brushed the necklace and cross that Fay had gifted to her when they had visited Tiffany's. She stopped, examined, the necklace, and admired it. "I do not recall this, Fay. Or the braids...for matter," Azrael said, confused.

"Let me start from the beginning. I promise you will understand." Fay grasped Azrael's left forearm. "Okay?"

Azrael nodded and remained silent.

"What I am about to tell you will sound unbelievable at first, but in the end, you will know what I have told you will make sense." Fay continued. "When we first met, you told me you are the namesake of the archangel Azrael."

Azrael confirmed, "I did say that."

"While you were sleeping in the cab, the archangel Azrael entered your body," Fay revealed. "She took your spirit and soul."

"I did not know it. Odd." Azrael appeared to reorganize her thought process. She then remarked,

"Cool!"

Fay was dumbfounded. *That's it?* she thought. *She believes me and thinks it's "cool?" Just like that?*

"Then what, ma'am?" Azrael prompted.

"Azrael had come to take me to the afterlife with her," Fay explained.

Azrael's expression reflected her concern. "Why? Were you in trouble for something you did, ma'am?"

Fay chuckled. "No. But I had cancer and she decided it was my time. But in the meantime, the angel hung around to help me out with Katrinka, to free her from prison, and as odd as it sounds, the angel wanted to take a break."

"She went on holiday?"

"Precisely. Well," Fay recapped, "during this time she got to know me and, at the same time, she had something for Katrinka to do for her."

"What?" Azrael asked.

"A part of it had to do with transporting conflict diamonds, and, as of yet, we don't know the reason why. And she wanted to convince Katrinka to choose to become the headship of the Romanov family."

"Did she, ma'am?"

"She did," Fay replied, "and she is now in Moscow."

Azrael rearranged herself on the sofa. "Then what?" she wondered.

Fay went on. "Well then, you, Azrael, made a deal with Katrinka. My soul for her agreeing to take the role of princess."

"It seems like a fair trade." Azrael briefly considered the deal. "But Kat did not want to be a princess. She wants to live in Seattle, become a nurse, yes?"

"Yes, but when I found out about the deal, I got mad. Like, 'over my dead body' mad." Fay reconciled her declaration for a second. "I now understand where the saying comes from."

'Wow!' Azrael exclaimed, as she listened to Fay recount the series of events that had led up until now. "So, I have been sleeping for weeks while the Angel of Death has been driving me around?"

"That's one way to put it," Fay replied.

Azrael again admired her necklace and cross. "You did not tell me where this came from, ma'am." She studied Fay with a measure of doubt evident on her face. "And don't tell me it came from heaven."

"The next best place," Fay quipped. "We were in Paris."

"France?"

"Yes, that Paris."

Azrael rubbed her head with her right hand as she processed the revelation. "Gosh. I am sorry I missed it."

"We took lots of memory photos on our cells. We can look at them sometime soon," Fay promised, before continuing, "We visited Tiffany's."

"The *Breakfast at Tiffany's*, Tiffany's?" Azrael gasped.

"One and the same." Fay held the necklace between her fingers as she admired it. "While we were there, you chose this necklace. The joy I saw on your face was to die for. And you had to have it!" Fay purposely did not say she had purchased the necklace as a gift for Azrael.

Azrael again admired the necklace. "It is beautiful." But she knew when things were just not right. She then said, "But I know myself, and I am too cheap to buy something this nice for myself." Azrael was growing more suspicious by the minute. "I think someone gave this to me. Right?" she guessed.

Fay nodded.

Azrael threw her arms around Fay. "It was you. Thank you, ma'am. You did not have to."

Fay smiled. "You are welcome. And I wanted to. You seem to like it as much now as you did then."

"It's one of the nicest things I have had in my life," Azrael gushed. "I am going to have to have the details. My mom will want to know everything. Where did I get it? How much did it cost? Did I use my college money to buy it? You know how moms are, ma'am. Once I clear all those questions, she will be ecstatic!"

Fay replied. "As it turns out, I am getting up to speed on the mom thing myself. Your mom will love it."

****

Kubinka Air Base Moscow Oblast, Russia

The Russian government's super-jet touched down on a cool, overcast early afternoon in the forest east of the Russian capital city. Once again, the two husky Russian men, who had turned out to be the pilots, carried Katrinka from the jet to the tarmac. There, a Russian soldier awaited Katrinka with a wheelchair. Sasha, Irishka, and two flight attendants followed with the luggage. A car waited, with its engine running, while the luggage and passengers were loaded aboard, although not before another series of selfies ensued. Katrinka loved every minute of it.

During the drive from Kubinka Air Base to Katrinka's apartment inside the Kremlin, which would serve as her safehouse and a temporary home-away-from-home, Sasha, Irishka, and Katrinka discussed her rudimentary staffing needs. It was decided Sasha would deal with secretarial needs and governmental functions, while Irishka considered the security needs. For the time being, the three agreed Katrinka would lay low while her foot continued to heal and an administrative assistant could be interviewed and hired. Katrinka eased down into the deep padding of the Mercedes rear passenger seat. With tears of sadness welling in her eyes, Russia's newest princess fell asleep.

****

Fay was pleasantly surprised by how quickly Azrael was adapting to her reintroduction to the world as she knew it. She decided to continue with Azrael's acclimation.

"I have some great news for you, Azrael," Fay said.

"Oh. I love great news." Azrael repositioned herself, folding her legs underneath her body. Intently, she gazed into Fay's eyes. "Okay! Lay it on me."

Fay loved Azrael's youthful enthusiasm. She was much the same as Katrinka in that way. "This evening," Fay explained, "we are going to SeaTac airport. You will be flying to LA to see your family."

Azrael screamed, probably louder than she had intended. "Alright!" she exclaimed. "Are you going with me?"

"No. I would like to, but I have to stay here and plan for what comes next," Fay replied.

Azrael pouted. "Too bad, ma'am. You would enjoy my family. I know they would love you!" she exclaimed.

"So, here's the deal," Fay told her. "I managed a seven-day leave extension for you. Sorry. While you are visiting with your family, the Marine Corps wants you to choose your next duty assignment."

Azrael continued to maintain her high level of enthusiasm. "My next duty?" she questioned warily.

"Yes," Fay informed her. "First Sergeant Grace wants you back at the U.S. Embassy."

"Cool!" Azrael replied. "I like First Sergeant."

Fay teased Azrael by adding, "Or…"

"Yeah, or?" Azrael questioned her. "Or what, ma'am?"

"Or," Fay answered, "there just so happens to be an opening on my team for an assistant."

Azrael hopped up as a wide smile formed on her lips. She then pretended to be weighing her two options. "I choose…I choose…?" She went back and forth. Finally, she said, "Ma'am, I am sorry to say…" She dragged her decision out as far as she could. "Ma'am, I want to join your team." She added, "Is it okay?"

Fay smiled. As she hugged Azrael, she said, "Welcome aboard, Corporal Lopez." Fay then clarified, "I must warn you, when you get back from LA, you are going to have only two days to prepare for our next six-month duty assignment aboard the U.S.S *Ronald Reagan*."

Azrael again screamed as she brought her hands to her mouth. Tears formed in her eyes. "A carrier!? How cool is that!"

"Very cool." Fay added, "Okay, let's get packed for your trip home." Then, noticing Azrael seemed tense, she asked, "You seem somewhat apprehensive.

Are you okay?"

"It's about my dream, ma'am." Azrael sipped at her milk then set the glass down. "A dream I had just before I woke up."

"Worth sharing?" Fay asked.

"Of course," Azrael responded. "Ma'am I was talking to people, but I did not know their language. But I could understand them and they could understand me." Azrael wrinkled her brow. "Weird, right?"

Fay had a thought. "You say you were speaking languages you do not know?" she repeated.

Azrael nodded.

"I wonder if you have remnants of the angel in your head?" Fay guessed. "Does it bother you?"

"No," Azrael replied, "it's interesting. I just wonder why I can speak and understand all of these languages?"

Chapter 14

Danilo Atienza Air Base lay eight miles south of Manila. It was the insufferable humidity that gave Fay pause about her decision to accept the six-month assignment aboard the U.S.S. *Ronald Reagan.* A Navy Grumman c-2 Greyhound propjet was being made ready to transport Fay and her team to the flight deck of the *Reagan.*

Fay counted a total of six passengers boarding the Greyhound. One attracted her notice: an odd woman. Fay's photographic memory nagged her about this particular seaman during the flight from Danilo Atienza Air Base. The landing on the *Reagan's* flight deck was rough, perhaps due to the gusty winds the pilots encountered. After the Greyhound's engines had stopped, the passengers were allowed to deplane. Fay, Don, and Azrael made their way to their quarters. Fay, opting not to dine in the customary officer's wardroom, agreed to meet her team in the crew mess for dinner.

It had been almost thirty hours of nonstop travel, with the exception of an overnight in Seoul. Fay was dead and slept from their arrival on the *Reagan* up to the dinner hour. She was dressing for dinner when a knock came on her stateroom door. She felt she was presentable enough to respond to the knock. It was her team, Lopez and Winslow, along with someone else, the odd passenger Fay had noticed on the flight.

Winslow introduced the woman to Fay. "Theodore, this is Commander Faydra Green." He then said to Fay, "Ma'am, this is Theodore."

Fay offered Theodore her hand. Theodore seemed hesitant and not quite sure whether she should salute or shake hands. With a little prompting from Fay, she shook. Yet, her grasp was very soft for a handshake.

All of this caused Fay to ask, "How did you guys meet Theodore?"

Winslow had an answer. "We found her wandering in the passageway, ma'am. She was lost."

Fay smiled. "Good catch, guys." It was then that Fay noticed Theodore's name plate. It read "Smith." Fay's investigative nature took over. She asked, "Is Theodore your first name?"

"Yes, ma'am," Theodore replied.

Theodore's response only served to open the door to many more questions. Yet, they all were hungry. Fay would get to the bottom of this double oddity later. She said to Theodore, "You will have dinner with us, won't you?"

Theodore again responded, "Yes, ma'am." Again, her answer lacked emotion or the warmth one would normally expect from a similar exchange.

Fay finished readying herself for dinner. Then, the four people made their way to the mess. Fay preceded Theodore through the serving line. About mid-point in the line, Fay noticed whenever she added something to her plate, Theodore would add the same thing to her own plate in an equal amount. Fay's curiosity demanded a test. When she got to the beverage dispensers, Fay served herself a one-half full glass of milk and then added a squirt of cola to it. She then observed Theodore, who did likewise. At this point, Fay was accumulating more questions about this odd sailor than an entire Sex-ed class of seventh graders would have about how exactly the human reproduction process worked.

Fay and her team found a table for four and sat. Whenever Fay did so much as lift her fork to eat peas, Theodore did the same in a complete imitation. Curious, Fay decided to test her hunch about Theodore. She asked, "Theodore, where are you from?"

Theodore placed her fork on her plate and responded, "*Deception Pass*, ma'am."

Bingo! Fay now knew something about Theodore. "You are a crew member aboard U.S.S. *Deception Pass*?" she asked, seeking clarity.

"Yes, ma'am," came the response.

Knowing this much, Fay reasoned if she continued to ask the other four thousand questions which were formulating in her mind, she and Theodore would be sitting there until sometime next week. However, Fay did say, "I have something for the three of you." She added, "Go with it, Don and Azrael."

Fay listed the names of roughly fifty percent of the former U.S. Presidents. She then asked Don, "Can you recite those names, past to present, back to me?" Don, who Fay was convinced held whiz-kid status, did get an impressive ninety percent correct. Next, Azrael tried. She too got roughly ninety percent right.

Next, it was Theodore's turn, but Fay asked the same question in a different way. "Theodore," she requested, "the names, please, in reverse order."

Theodore began her task. When she had completed it, she scored not only one hundred percent correct but had included the Vice Presidents as well, even though Fay had not listed them.

"Great job, all of you!" Fay praised her group. She had an award for Theodore. "You and I are going for dessert," she told Theodore. "What I want you to do is to serve yourself double of my serving." She smiled. "Got it?"

Theodore did smile, which up to this point she had not done. This indicated to Fay there was, at the very least, some hint of life going on in Theodore's odd mind.

Following dinner, Fay and team returned to Fay's stateroom. Fay asked Theodore to sit in a nearby chair. Then, she told Don and Azrael, "We have a serious problem. Theodore is not supposed to be on this ship. I don't yet know how or why, but until I get some answers, will one of you volunteer to keep an eye on her for me?"

Azrael was quick to answer. "I will, ma'am."

Fay smiled. "Are you sure? This is complicated. I know you can handle it. Do you want the job?"

Azrael turned her attention to Theodore. "Yes, ma'am. I'm up for it." She returned her attention to Fay. "It's like being a babysitter I think, ma'am."

Fay offered an appreciative nod. "That is one way to put it." She then asked, "Will you and Don escort her to her bunk and get her settled for the night?"

"They have her in a stateroom, ma'am," Winslow clarified.

"A stateroom?"

Winslow nodded, affirmative.

The list of questions was mounting. "Okay," Fay replied. "When you get her settled, meet me back here.

We need to talk." Fay looked again at Theodore. She said to Don and Azrael, "You two may well have saved this young woman's life today."

****

Kremlin, Moscow, Russia, the same day

His name was Bradley Lee, but he preferred to be known as "Buddy." Katrinka had chosen him from among those she had interviewed for her assistant role. She chose Buddy because he was an American approximately her age. He had lived in America for most of his life before moving to Russia. His parents were both Russian. He had joined the Russian Navy as an officer candidate. He told Katrinka he had graduated from a university she did not know, Boston College, with a degree in computer science. Well, it was not important anyway. What was important to her was his English was flawless. One of her life's goals was to perfect her English fluency. And Buddy was someone who could help her achieve this goal.

Katrinka's apartment was adequate. Like much of the Kremlin, it was old. Her home was recently restored, and it had the flavor of old Russia in its architecture, with its super high ceiling, doors, and windows. If she were to use an adjective, "grand" would be the word of choice - according to Buddy, anyway.

Kat could come and go as she pleased - provided, for her protection, someone escorted her. It could be Sasha, Irishka, or Buddy. Although Buddy, unlike Sasha and Irishka, was not Navy military special forces, he was still a large fellow, and according to him, he was experienced in martial arts and had some kind of belt thingy to prove it. She too had received training in martial arts while attending the Russian government sponsored spy school. Buddy was curious about her spy school martial arts training. She explained to him she was taught Systema, a combat method dating back to the time of the Cossacks. At a later time, this method had been taught to KBG agents and Soviet Spetsnaz (special forces). Katrinka and Buddy were formidable as a duo. When her foot had mended, Kat put Buddy on notice she planned to find out which of their two practices was more effective. What may turn out to be the battle of the century was on a future fight card. Katrinka's take on the matter: Buddy had best be ready to get his ass kicked by a girl.

Although she was not worried about it, she did consider the fact her Kremlin housing was government controlled. Her assistant was a Russian naval officer. Her apartment may be bugged and her conversations monitored. To this point, the Russian government had not taken an overt interest in her, yet she knew she needed to distance herself from any political influence if she hoped to gain the trust of the Russian people as their advocate. She considered settling in Vladivostok because it was a large city located as far from Moscow as possible. Vladivostok was dreadfully cold in the winter months but beautiful in the summer months. She reasoned she would have the financial means to move around with the intent of always living in a warmer climate. Sochi…or Seattle, if possible?

****

U.S.S. Ronald Reagan, South China Sea

Fay and her team had reconvened in her stateroom. Fay's concern was focused on Theodore. She began by saying, "Theodore is a crew member of the U.S.S.

Deception Pass." She looked at Don and Azrael to emphasize her next declaration. "Much of *Deception Pass's* importance to the Navy is top-secret. I have to be careful what I say in that regard."

"We understand, ma'am," Winslow confirmed.

"Let me put it this way," Fay elaborated. "Don, I want you to go online and search the term "Philadelphia Experiment" on the official Navy website. I know you know about the experiment, but I want you and Azrael to be on the same page with what I am about to say."

Don got busy on his laptop accessing the Navy official website. While Don and Azrael perused the website, Fay went for coffee.

When Fay had returned, Azrael began summarizing as she recited over Don's shoulder. "The *Eldridge* was a destroyer, ma'am. The Navy created technology which would make the *Eldridge* disappear. They could move it to another location where it then would reappear."

Fay took a sip from her cup and nodded. "Teleporting. For lack of a better description, the purpose of the *Eldridge.*"

Winslow ventured a guess. "The experiments continued and now we have the U.S.S. *Deception Pass*?"

Fay continued without confirming. "All ships in our Navy have a crew." Fay had been aboard *Deception Pass* in the past year. She was aware of her capabilities. The ship could both appear and disappear but also had the capability of limited time travel. Fay herself had traveled aboard the ship into the past. None of this she could discuss with Don and Azrael in detail.

Don put it together. "Theodore is a *Deception Pass*

crew member."

Fay said, "Anyway, I wanted you guys to know about the *Eldridge*. Interesting, is it not?"

Don and Azrael both nodded in agreement.

Fay asked, "Both of you have noticed Theodore is seriously lacking in social skills while at the same time being highly intelligent, right?"

"Yeah, that was amazing she could recite the past presidents backwards without batting an eye," Don recalled. "She is somewhat like a human version of a dolphin."

Fay had not considered Don's interesting comparison. As a further demonstration of Theodore's intellect, Fay told the others, "I asked her what the square root of five was. None of us would know the answer. Would we?"

"I think it will be in the two and change range?" Whiz kid Winslow guessed.

At this point, Azrael's eyes had crossed.

"Without a calculator," Fay recalled, "Theodore told me 'two point two three and six, ma'am.' Then she added, 'there are more numbers, ma'am, so if you need them, I will tell you. But it is close enough.'"

"Theodore is a computer," Azrael offered.

"Android?" Winslow guessed.

Fay wrinkled her brow as she sipped at her coffee. "I don't know. What I do know is she is on the wrong ship. Why is she here, and if she needs to be on *Deception Pass,* how do we get her there?"

Fay glanced at her wristwatch. "In forty minutes, I am to attend a meeting in the captain's quarters. I am going to be introduced to his senior crew." Turning to allow them both to evaluate her, she added, "How do I look?"

"As beautiful as ever, ma'am," Azrael confirmed.

"I will pull the captain aside and make him aware of Theodore and the challenges and liabilities he is faced with," Fay resolved.

****

21:45 hours, the Captain's Reception

Fay was introduced by Captain Calvin "Clem" Clemson to his officers and staff. Some knew of her father or had actually met him. And, of course, all were impressed a Navy carrier, the U.S.S. *William R. Green*, bore her family name.

While Fay enjoyed the various conversations, she did wish to speak to Captain Clemson regarding Theodore. She saw the captain standing alone. She approached him. "I want to thank you, sir, for the warm reception," Fay began.

"We are happy to have you aboard, Commander Green," Captain Clemson responded. "If there is anything I can do to make your stay more pleasant, please, let me know."

"Captain, I do have something I wanted to make you aware of," Fay disclosed.

"Oh?" he curiously responded.

"Sir, today I met a woman who seems to be on the wrong ship."

Captain Clemson's eyebrows arched. With concern, he asked, "Commander, can we step aside? My inner office?" he suggested.

He motioned Fay toward an open door which accessed his office. Inside, three or four officers were having a discussion. He asked them to excuse him. They obliged and left to continue their discussion elsewhere.

"Please, have a seat," Clemson offered.

Fay smiled. They both sat.

Fay began speaking. "This afternoon, my Legalman found a sailor wandering lost in a passageway. Based on my conversation with her, I do know she is not assigned to the *Reagan.*"

Immediately, Captain Clemson cut to the chase, a quality which Fay herself possessed and admired in others. He asked, "We will want to know how and why. Where do you recommend we begin.

Chapter 15

It was going to be a big day for Russia's President Rudkovsky. He had a scheduled meeting with Russia's heir apparent to the royal headship of Russia, Lady Yekaterina.

Katrinka shared with Buddy, "President must be really excited to meet me."

Irishka, Sasha, and Buddy would accompany Kat to the small lunch hour gathering - a "meet and greet," as Buddy called it.

"What to wear to meet and greet?" Katrinka asked Irishka the day prior to the meeting. "I have blue jeans."

Irishka promised a trip to the Red Square across from the Kremlin for shopping. Katrinka protested, "I am a doer. Not a shopper!"

Irishka assured Kat the excursion would be relatively painless. Irishka glanced at her wristwatch. "We must go now," she urged. "Meeting is tomorrow."

Irishka, Buddy, and Katrinka went shopping. The adventure turned out to be short and sweet.

"No dress. They reminded me of sparrow," Katrinka protested. "No high shoes. Stilettos make me appear ten feet tall." She did concede one point. "Make up is okay."

The "Blue Jean Princess," as Buddy called her, eventually settled on a dark suit and black flats. As an aside, Katrinka wondered why anyone in their right mind would pay big money for blue jean with rips and tears in them.

"You are going to put serious dent in Russia's fashion industry," Irishka warned Kat. "What you wear, all women will wear," she predicted.

****

Fay enjoyed the selfies sent to her by Katrinka. She thought Kat looked regal in her suit. But she was reminded again how much Irishka and Katrinka resembled one another. Buddy Lee was a handsome lad, she thought. Azrael agreed with Fay. Winslow looked at Buddy's picture too, but he was mum on the subject.

Fay and her staff had agreed to meet prior to breakfast. Winslow and Azrael had also promised to meet Theodore in thirty minutes. Fay shared with them the details of her meeting the prior evening with Captain Clemson. He had had a crewman verify Seaman Smith's purpose aboard the *Reagan*. Clemson was told Theodore was to have arrived with a second sailor. The two of them were to rendezvous with a chopper sent by *Deception Pass* to ferry them from the *Reagan* to their duty stations. Something had gone wrong. Seaman Smith was not to have traveled without an escort.

"Guys, Theodore has no purpose for being on this ship," Fay told her staff. "A fear I shared with the captain was, if she were left unattended, problems could occur. So, until the chopper arrives, I volunteered us to assist her." Fay smiled. "This means she will spend her days aboard ship with us."

"We are here to help, ma'am," Winslow assured Fay.

Following breakfast, Winslow quickly discovered

Theodore was adept at researching any topic. She seemed most content when the assigned task had a high degree of difficulty associated with it. During the first day, they learned if someone were to visit the office with a question or complex series of instructions, and if Theodore were listening, she could recite verbatim the discussion which occurred.

This prompted Winslow to observe, "Theodore is not only a computer, she's a voice recorder as well."

Fay told Don and Azrael, and they agreed: Theodore was the most intelligent person they had ever met. They speculated Theodore's IQ would be off the charts.

"She's like a double Einstein," Azrael noted.

Fay had commented on the matter before when she again said to Don and Azrael, "For however smart she is, she is sorely lacking in social skills."

Azrael's curiosity about Theodore's evident brilliance caused her to wonder why one could be so smart and yet so lacking in some social skills. An internet search revealed information about individuals who were known as "savants." She told Fay and Don, "Theodore, as a savant, could either have a high IQ or a low IQ. Seems she has the high version." Azrael went on to inform them, "A savant now living in Nebraska has memorized the Holy Bible. Another, after hearing piano music played on the radio, later that day sat at a piano at home and proceeded to play the tune. It was Tchaikovsky's Piano Concerto No. 1."

"Wow," Fay lamented. "You know, I don't want us to assume our Theodore is a savant. Because how would she have been allowed into the Navy?" Fay reviewed her thoughts and then speculated, "Unless our

Navy in its sometimes misguided purposes has found our savant brothers and sisters are well suited for special purpose duty aboard the *Deception Pass*?" Fay qualified her next statement by saying, "My choice of comparison is poor at best, but it is the only one I can think of at the moment. It reminds me of dolphins and how the Navy utilizes those intelligent creatures."

Don added, "In a way, this is horrible. Dolphins have handlers who manage their Navy lives. Our dolphins even hold rank. The two who saved your life, ma'am, a few years back were promoted as a result."

"Yes," Fay replied softly. "You are suggesting, and you could be correct, Theodore and her fellow crew aboard the *Deception Pass* are..." Fay could not complete her thought. She then said, "I seldom find myself at a loss. Yet, I am so conflicted on this right now. I just don't know." Fay turned to Don. "Will you help Corporal Lopez gain access to our systems? User ID, passwords, whatever else?"

"Sure, ma'am," Winslow responded.

"Then teach Lopez how to access personnel records," Fay said. "I need to get ahold of who Theodore reports to and find out what is going on."

"We're on it, ma'am," Winslow assured her.

Fay noticed although Theodore was an interesting conversationalist, she did not initiate exchanges. She was a "speak only when spoken to" person. Theodore was somewhat like Winslow in that she had knowledge spanning a wide range of diverse topics.

****

The Ceremonial Drawing Room was large and ornate. President Rudkovsky and several of his top staff were in attendance. Buddy, Irishka, and Sasha accompanied Katrinka. The furnishings were vintage, as was a gold samovar so large, it almost dominated the room. There were several balalaika musicians and three or four waitpersons, all dressed in early twentieth century traditional Russian costumes. The focal point of the drawing room was a crystal chandelier, which appeared to Katrinka to be equivalent in size to a small car.

Pointing toward the chandelier, Katrinka commented to Buddy, "The cleaning bill on that thing must be huge."

Buddy estimated, "I bet. It would take a nine-meter ladder just to reach it."

Katrinka and President Rudkovsky were seated in two side-by-side wingback chairs placed in front of a grand marble fireplace and arranged in the standard head of state meeting photo op configuration. As they chatted, a photographer and a videographer recorded the event. This meeting was a precursor to be the grand gala planned for Katrinka's introduction to the people of Russia, scheduled for six months later.

****

Theodore was a talkative person and intensely inquisitive. She surprised Fay when she asked, "Ma'am, I read the paper you published while you attended law school at the University of Texas. It was interesting when you discussed your proposed standards of liability with regard to autonomous machines."

Fay replied, "What was your conclusion? Agree or disagree?"

"I somewhat agree, but you could have gone deeper into your proposal on artificial intelligence and robots," Theodore explained.

"How so?" Fay queried.

"Androids, ma'am." Theodore continued her train of thought. "In the nineteen fifties, Isaac Asimov wrote 'Hardwired.' Do you know it?"

"I do," Fay replied. "I cited Asimov several times in my paper."

"I noticed, ma'am," Theodore responded. "At the time, I wondered when self-awareness, artificial intelligence, and robotics would merge." She then changed the topic. "Ma'am, why did you not pursue a Ph.D.?"

"I decided to join the Navy."

"Oh," Theodore said thoughtfully.

"Suppose technology evolves to the point where, as Asimov suggested, autonomy and artificial intelligence allow for an android society?" Fay asked. "Will androids and humans have equal rights?"

Theodore had an answer. "I would expect it, ma'am. Once a machine can make decisions then in turn it must be responsible for its actions. Just as humans arc."

"Human laws will apply to machines?" Fay wondered.

Theodore explained, "If a machine broke a civil law or criminal law, then one would reason a free-thinking machine would also be responsible for it actions. Just as a human would."

Fay was enjoying her debate with Theodore. "But who is held responsible for the machine's actions?" she queried.

"Your paper proposed it, ma'am," Theodore reminded her. "Which is why I said you should take your proposed standards of liability further. We have no laws governing machine law."

Winslow, who was sitting nearby, now interjected, "I've overheard your conversations. Do you mind if I join?"

"Join in, Don," Fay welcomed him.

"Your discussion with regard to liability got my attention," Don informed them. "May I ask, if an autonomous machine did break a law, who is liable?"

"My paper asked this," Fay replied, "as a rhetorical question. Because we do not have new laws addressing the question, we do not have an answer," she explained. "If an autonomous machine causes an injury, be it accidental or intentional, for example, who would be held liable should a lawsuit surface?"

"I see," Don said. "The question is then would it be either the machine, the programmer of the machine, or the manufacturer of the machine? Or any combination of the three?"

"Precisely," Fay stated. "It was my argument, anyway."

"Theodore," Don asked, "will we see the day of the *Terminator*?"

Theodore answered, "Humans cannot co-exist in many cases in many times. They war. Why would an artificial intelligence not as well?"

Fay glanced at her wristwatch. Then, she told Winslow, "I think you would find the bridge interesting. So, Don, you are with me." She paused, then announced, "Okay, y'all, I have a meeting with Captain Clemson. I hope to learn for how much longer Theodore will be with us. In the meantime, Azrael, the XO seems to think we are the most creative team onboard this week. He has requested we plan a small birthday party for Captain Clemson." With a look of hope on her face, Fay asked, "What do you think? Doable?"

"Thanks, ma'am," Azrael replied. "Theodore and I will give it a try."

Fay smiled. "You two will do just fine," she encouraged. "Tiny, small, teeny party. Okay?"

While Fay and Winslow were away, Azrael and Theodore began their planning. When fifteen minutes had passed and neither woman had an idea to share between them, Theodore revealed, "I've never planned a party before. I have no clue where to begin."

Azrael had an idea. "Theodore, you play musical instruments, right?"

"I do," Theodore confirmed. "Maybe twenty or so?"

"And you are a mimic. Right?"

Theodore repeated the instructions Fay had given them not twenty minutes prior: "Okay, y'all, I have a meeting with Captain Clemson. I hope to learn for how much longer Theodore will be with us. In the meantime, Azrael, the XO seems to think we are the most creative team on board this week. He has requested we plan a small birthday party for Captain Clemson."

An astonished Azrael responded, "That is unreal! You sound exactly like her!"

Theodore smiled. She seemed pleased with herself.

"I have an idea," Azrael stated. "Let's get out a notice to the crew we are looking for a few rock musicians. We will put a band together. You provide vocals and guitar," she suggested to Theodore.

"I can do that. But I need to hear the musical

arrangements."

"I think the X-O included a playlist of the captain's favorite music in the party instructions." Azrael scooted across the office on her office chair, grabbed a file from a nearby desk, and then scooted back to Theodore. Her eager eyes scanned the pages. "There!" she exclaimed, pointing to an entry midway down a page. "Classic rock! Captain likes classic rock." She continued to read. "Let's see…lots of good music here." She looked up from the list at Theodore. "Raven! He likes Raven!"

"I can do Raven," a confident Theodore confirmed.

"We'll get a cover band together for a gig on the hanger deck tomorrow night." Azrael asked with hope in her eyes, "Sound good?"

"Sounds good," Theodore responded. "I will learn her songs and study how she moves. I can be ready by tomorrow night."

Azrael's creative side took over. "I see a large cake shaped like an aircraft carrier. It has gray frosting. The hangar deck, a stage. The show is scheduled to begin at nineteen-thirty hours. Everyone is waiting with anticipation for Raven and her group. But she is late. The excitement is building. At nineteen forty, a chopper descends on the lift from the flight deck, like you just flew in from somewhere. Lots of flashing lights!"

Theodore seemed lost in the dream as she listened to Azrael describe the event.

"The lift stops. The band emerges. Lights are flashing. Everyone is going nuts!" Azrael took a breath. Her surveying eyes studied Theodore for an instant. "We can do some hair. Make up. I can put together an outfit." Azrael paused. "You still with me?" she asked Theodore.

"I can do it," she assured Azrael.

"If you are as good as I think you will be, I bet half of the crew will believe they are seeing Raven," Azrael proclaimed. "The other half won't be as sure."

"What about you?" Theodore asked.

"What? Who, me? The Chicana from East LA?"

"So, like, um, you're going to like totally blow off your shot at like fun and fame, girlfriend?" Theodore quipped.

Azrael laughed. "You do Valley really well!"

Chapter 16

It is said trouble travels in threes. The captain's party was a ripping success. The majority of the crew bought into Theodore's cover band performance of Raven. The captain had just enough beer to drink by the time he met Theodore and Azrael after the performance to believe he had actually met Raven. Winslow told the team the show was streamed to the five ships in the task force, who in turn streamed the show to any ship or island in the Pacific Fleet who could get reception. Don estimated over 130,000 crewmembers enjoyed Theodore and Azrael's rendition of the universal recording sensation via video relays.

It began when Fay received Azrael's frantic call. "Ma'am!" Azrael cried. "I've lost Theodore!"

"Slow down, sweetie," Fay responded in a calming voice. "How did we lose her?"

"Ma'am, we were walking from the hangar deck to the flight deck," Azrael said breathlessly, "with a shore patrol detail. I was walking ahead, but she was talking to me. Mid-sentence she screamed. Small scream," Azrael clarified. "I turned and she was gone!"

"How gone?" Fay asked.

"Gone, gone, ma'am," Azrael expounded. "Really gone, ma'am."

"Okay. She is somewhere. Meet Don and I at my stateroom," Fay instructed.

****

Two small bomb blasts erupted near Saint Basil's Cathedral sixty minutes after the historic Kremlin meeting between Princess Yekaterina and Russian President Rudkovsky. A family was injured in the explosions.

"And so it begins," a saddened Sasha said to his comrade Irishka.

"The communist party has claimed responsibility," Irishka said. "First there are gunshots near her room in Paris. Then car tries to run her over. Is warning of more to come," she predicted.

"President Rudkovsky has admonished the perpetrators," Sasha informed Irishka and Buddy.

"Katrinka is concerned and wants to visit the family at the hospital," Irishka responded.

"Would it be wise for her to do so?" Buddy asked.

"She will be safe," Irishka assured him. "Better if we travel now. She must appear unaffected by this," she advised.

"Where is she?" Sasha asked.

"In her bedroom. She is taking nap," Irishka said. "I will wake her."

"I will call Faya," Sasha offered.

****

Sasha's call, while welcome, was also distressing. Yet, he was able to assure Fay everything would be alright. Sasha texted the photos of Katrinka's meeting with President Rudkovsky and she streamed the concert to Sasha. Not long after, Azrael arrived. She was visibly upset.

"Ma'am, she disappeared!" Azrael exclaimed.

"And where is Don?" Fay asked her.

"He said he would be here. I don't know where he is!"

"Okay. Let's sit," Fay said. "We will figure this out. By the way, Lopez, the captain sends his regards. That was a heck of a party you put on. Congratulations!" Fay then recollected her thoughts. "Lopez?" she asked, after a brief pause.

"Yes, ma'am?"

"When Don and I left this office to visit the bridge, I recall leaving instructions for you and Theodore. I recall the words 'small,' 'tiny,' and 'teeny' as the operative words in those instructions. Did you two miss that part of the instructions?"

"Yes, ma'am," Azrael sheepishly replied.

Fay smiled. "A good thing it turned out to be a huge success, wasn't it?"

Don arrived several minutes later. He too appeared as frantic as Azrael.

"Ma'am, the Master at Arms aboard the U.S.S. *Brittany Michael* contacted us," Winslow reported.

Fay's first concern was to bring a sense of calm to her two mildly upset charges. "Let's all relax and practice the breathing exercise we learned," she suggested.

When all were comfortable, Fay closed her eyes and said, "Eyes closed. Let's take big, deep breaths."

Don and Azrael did as Fay said.

"As we breathe in, let's imagine the air is filled with calm and peace. And we are going to feel it fill our bodies." As they breathed, Fay instructed, "When we breathe out, we are going to say in our minds, 'I breathe out my stress and tension.'"

Fay, Don, and Azrael all continued breathing,

conducting the exercise for less than a minute. "Alright!" Fay announced. "Let's tackle this again." She looked toward Don. "Tell us about *Brittany Michael*."

"Ma'am, a sailor is being held. According to the Master at Arms, there was disagreement between two sailors. One has died," Winslow reported.

Fay held her gaze on Don. "And Theodore has seemingly vanished."

"That's what I understand, ma'am," Winslow confirmed.

Fay had a theory regarding Theodore's disappearance but was unable to share it with them because of the secret nature of the U.S.S. *Deception Pass*. She had given them a few clues, however. Don and Azrael would have to work with those.

Fay quickly formulated a game plan. "Don, you and Azrael put your heads together," she ordered. "Come up with a short list of your initial thoughts on how to go about finding our missing friend." Fay rose from her chair. "I need coffee." She considered. "And vodka, I think."

Don and Azrael went to work organizing their thoughts. Fay returned to her desk with the coffee. "I will contact the Master at Arms on the U.S.S. *Michael*," she decided. "Do we have a name, Donald?"

"Lieutenant Zeigler, ma'am," Winslow replied. He handed her a slip of paper. "Here is the contact information."

Fay surveyed the document. "I am going to access the service records of Seaman Leeci Chen and Seaman Jamie Dean, while the two of you find Theodore." Fay glanced again at the document. "What are your initial thoughts?" she asked Don and Azrael.

"We are going to access the service records and interview the five-person shore patrol detail who accompanied Azrael and Theodore from the hangar deck to the flight deck," Winslow said.

"Wait," Azrael said with a hint of doubt in her voice. "There were six shore patrol. Not five. I am certain of my count."

Winslow reviewed his notes. "I have five names on the detail req."

"Am I hearing we are missing not only our Theodore but a shore patrolman as well?" Fay queried.

"The list does not match our head count, ma'am," Azrael confirmed.

By late morning, Azrael and Winslow had contacted the five sailors who had escorted Azrael and Theodore from the concert stage to the flight deck. Their accountings of the disappearance all matched. She and a shore patrolman they did not know had disappeared. Don viewed what video he could find of the group's travels from the stage area to the flight deck. There wasn't a record of the moments surrounding the disappearance.

Meanwhile, Fay had contacted the Master at Arms aboard the U.S.S. *Michael*. Lieutenant Zeigler had confined Seaman Chen to quarters pending Fay's interview and investigation. This meant Fay would be required to travel from the *Reagan* to the *Michael*.

Winslow arranged for her transfer. "Don, please tell me small boats, lifelines, or ropes dangling from choppers will not be in my future when I travel to the *Michael*," Fay pleaded.

"No, ma'am." Winslow assured her. "The *Michael*

has a helo pad."

Fay felt because Seaman Chen was a woman, it would be less threating if she and Azrael met with her. Winslow would continue investigating Theodore's disappearance.

****

U.S.S. Brittany Michael, Yellow Sea, Pacific Ocean

"Seaman Chen," Fay began. "I'm the task force JAG. My assistant Corporal Lopez and I have been assigned to conduct a preliminary investigation into the death of Seaman Dean. I am required by military law to advise you of your rights. Article Fifteen and Article Thirty-one of the UCMJ gives you those rights. I would like to ask you some questions, but I want to advise you that you have the right to remain silent. That means you have the right to say nothing at all. Any statement you do make, either oral or written, may be used against you in a trial by courts-martial or in any other proceedings." Fay continued, "You have the right to consult with a lawyer before any questioning. Unfortunately, it means we would suspend you from duty until we reach a port. With that said, I will inquire if we are allowed, and if needed, a Zoom meeting with a civilian lawyer. You are allowed to have a lawyer present during this or any other interview. You can have military representation free of charge. In addition to military counsel, you are entitled to civilian counsel at your own expense. You may request a lawyer anytime someone is interviewing you. Have you requested counsel?"

"No," Leeci replied.

"If you decide to answer my questions or anyone else's questions, you can stop the questioning at any time," Fay informed her. "Do you understand your rights as provided by Articles Fifteen and Thirty-one?"

"I do."

"Do you want a lawyer at this time?"

"No. I want to talk to you, Commander Green. I called my dad," Leeci explained. "He told me to talk only to you."

"Did your father serve?" Fay inquired.

"Yes, ma'am. I am second generation Navy," Leeci said, with a measure of pride evident in her voice.

"Are you willing to answer my questions then?"

"Yes, ma'am."

Fay smiled at Leeci. "Corporal Lopez and I are both going to record our discussion on our tablets. Don't let it concern you. Any information we notate will be kept confidential." Fay looked to Leeci for her approval. "You good?"

Leeci agreed, "Okay."

"We are going to enter today's time and date, plus your full name, your rank, and your duty assignment. So, let's begin with your full name."

"Leeci Mary Chen. Seaman. Cryptologic Technician Technical CTT. U.S.S. *Brittany Michael*," came the answer.

"Your technical training was in my hometown, Leeci," Fay noted.

"Pensacola is a nice area, ma'am."

Fay read from the Master at Arms' report. "Lieutenant Zeigler says you told him Seaman Dean fell. He struck his head. Is that accurate, Leeci?" she asked.

Leeci's eyes flooded with tears. She tried to speak but was unable to. Azrael offered her a tissue. Fay waited while Leeci regained her composure. "Why don't we have Corporal Lopez get you a glass of water," Fay offered.

When Azrael returned with the water, Fay waited for a few more moments and then began again. "Seaman Dean fell. Blunt force trauma resulted in his death."

Leeci nodded in agreement.

A sympathetic Fay said, "Can you tell me what happened?"

Leeci nodded, sniffed, blew her nose, and took a sip of water. "Jamie and I had watched the concert, ma'am."

Fay confirmed, "The one from the *Reagan*. Correct?"

"Several of us had a small party. We had snacks and drank beer." Leeci paused to refresh herself. "Jamie must have had more beer than he had intended. He tried to kiss me. I did not want hm too." She paused again. "Well, I wanted him too but not then." She looked to Fay and Azrael. "You know what I mean?"

Both Fay and Azrael offered understanding nods.

"Go on," Fay said.

"So, I pushed him away from me. It was playful, but too hard, I think, because he fell backward. He hit his head on a table and fell down." Leeci broke into tears. "I am so sorry, ma'am. Jamie was a good guy. He did not deserve this. I am so sorry."

Fay thought it best to suspend Leeci's accounting of the incident. "Leeci, sit tight while Corporal Lopez and I conference," she requested. "Okay?"

Leeci nodded in agreement.

Fay and Azrael left the room. In the passageway,

Fay asked, "What do you think?"

"I think Seaman Chen is unfortunate," Azrael replied. "This appears to be an accident. She is a sweet and kind lady."

"And what does your intuition tell you, Corporal?" Fay asked.

Azrael paused for a moment to collect her thoughts. "Seaman Chen is a sweet and kind lady. This should not have happened."

Fay then asked, "What does your heart tell you?"

"We must help her, ma'am."

Fay smiled. She patted Azrael on her right shoulder. "Good job. You and I think alike."

Azrael smiled. "Thank you, ma'am. You don't know how much your vote of confidence means to me." Azrael hesitated, "Ma'am, can we take her back to the *Reagan* with us?"

"Why do you say that?" Fay wondered.

"Scuttlebutt, ma'am. It may be unkind, and it will only serve to confirm in her mind she has done something more wrong than she really has." Azrael was concerned. "She may become harmful to herself."

Fay smiled again. "I like the way you think, Corporal. Would you be willing to supervisor her if I can get her over to the *Reagan* with us?"

"Of course!" Azrael volunteered. Sheepishly, she added, "I don't suppose I could lose two people? Could I?"

"Don't beat yourself up over it." Fay added a reassuring smile, "Winslow will find Theodore. Let's go back inside. We'll see what Leeci thinks."

Fay and Azrael returned to the room. Leeci seemed to have recovered, at least measurably, anyway.

"Seaman Chen," Fay began. "We have not yet considered all of your options, but we do feel you should move to the *Reagan* to be with us." Fay offered a reassuring smile. "Would you like that?"

Leeci did not hesitate. "Yes, ma'am! Is it possible?"

"I can make it happen. I will talk to Lieutenant Zeigler about it. Why don't you and Azrael get your gear and then meet back here?" Fay suggested.

Azrael and a remarkably happier Leeci left the room. Fay contacted the Master at Arms. He realized the logic to her request and agreed to the transfer. By the time Azrael and Leeci returned, Fay told them the news.

Chapter 17

Kremlyovka Hospital, Moscow, Russia

The weather was angry this day. It could often be so in the Russian city if one had the mood to match. Katrinka spent her day visiting with the family who had been involved in the bombing in the Red Square. She enjoyed playing with the two children who had been injured and conversing with their parents. The Russian media learned of the visit and were on hand to record Russia's new royal as she endeared herself to both the patients and staff of Kremlyovka. Yuri Orlov had moved his family to Moscow from Tula when the economy had closed the electric plant where he had worked. They had little money and Yuri was having difficulty finding employment. The injuries only added to their troubles. Katrinka learned both Yuri and his wife Marina had deferred their own medical needs to those of their children, something all too common for their Russian parent counterparts. Marina was in need of extensive dental surgery, while Yuri had nerve damage to his back and legs as a result of job-related accident. Both parents also were in need of glasses.

While Katrina and Irishka met with the Orlov family, Katrinka sent Buddy Lee to find an apartment near the hospital. Buddy secured and paid for a one-year lease for the apartment, which included utilities.

Katrinka also arranged with the hospital to cover any medical expenses incurred by the family not covered by the Russian health care system. Using her new royal family letterhead, she presented a letter of recommendation to Yuri signed by her, which Yuri could present to a potential employer during his job search. She may as well put the ninety million plus to good use, she reasoned.

The angel Azrael had warned Katrinka to beware of the demon Mazikim. Azrael had told her Mazikim had been responsible for Rasputin, the mystic and self-proclaimed holy man who was the advisor to the last empress consort of Russia, Alexandra Feodorovna, her great-great grandmother, approximately.

Not in Katrinka's life had she experienced the emotion of anger. Nor did she allow for herself to become upset. On this day, she found herself upset she had allowed herself to become angry. Someone had purposefully staged a bombing, in protest of her ascendancy to the crown, that resulted in the injuries of good and innocent people. In her mind, this was absolutely unacceptable.

The Russian media reported a militant faction of the communist party had taken credit for the blast. Katrinka believed this would not be the last time. If Mazikim was an influence, then Mazikim must be stopped. Azrael the angel had told her when an angel assumed a human form, the angel was as vulnerable to harm as any human. She had managed to kill the archangel Gabriel by mistake. How was a girl to know? Unless Mazikim revealed herself, Katrinka would not know her from anyone else. For the time being, Katrinka's newfound anger was directing traffic.

****

U.S.S. Ronald Reagan, on duty, South China Sea

Fay had made an agreement with the U.S.S. *Michael* Master at Arms Lieutenant Zeigler allowing JAG Corps to assume responsibility for Leeci Chen. It helped in her proposal to Zeigler to note Corporal Lopez's duty assignment was Embassy Security and Corporal Lopez would be specifically responsible for Seaman Chen. It would be Fay's job to continue an investigation into the death of the sailor and then make a recommendation to the captain of the *Michael*. The two most likely options were either a captain's mast or a court martial procedure.

Up to now, Fay had experienced a high degree of success in the courtroom. Foremost was her successful defense of three Marines accused of murder and their subsequent acquittal. Another win she was not proud of was her successful defense of the son of a mafia crime boss accused of armed robbery. Ultimately, the case had contributed to the part she had played in setting up the Justice Department's successful win in a major anti-trust case. She worried about this one and did not understand why. Perhaps her experience with the Angel of Death and her now cured cancer served to make her realize she was not as infallible as she once believed? Was she losing her edge? Her belief going forward was she was going to do her best to assure Leeci received every consideration in her upcoming hearing. Her first step was to control the series of events that would lead to the hearing. To accomplish this, the ball must remain in her court.

Theodore had not been found. During the afternoon, Winslow arrived with the usual afternoon mail. The mail included a large bowling ball sized box addressed to Azrael. Azrael assumed it was cookies from her parents as she ripped open the box. Fay and Winslow returned to their work.

"Eek!" Azrael shrieked.

"Eeks" were not a part of Azrael's vocabulary. Winslow commented to Fay, "Must be either a spider or a snake." Both turned their attention to Azrael, who was staring into the box.

"It's Theodore," she informed them. She added, "She returned my blue jeans, shoes she wore during the concert, and an envelope."

First, mystery solved. The stamp on the box indicated it had been shipped from the *Deception Pass*. Fay's suspicion was confirmed. Because the *Deception Pass* could teleport with crew included, it stood to reason the Navy had developed a means to do the same with her crew without the ship being included.

Azrael added, "There is a letter." She ripped open the letter. "It's the necklace I loaned her. The one I got at Tiffany's. Theodore writes, 'Like, the best time ever, girlfriend. Love you. Theodore.'" She turned to Fay and Winslow. "She is safe! So cool!"

From their first week aboard the *Reagan,* Azrael and Theodore had been taking an interest in the study of the Holy Bible. They began attending weekly Bible study meetings, but not about one religion. Rather, they would often attend two different meetings, one a non-denominational meeting and one about the Jewish faith. Fay wondered what had prompted this new interest. Could the angel have left a remnant of her spirit in Azrael which was now manifesting itself in her mortal soul? Azrael invited Leeci to join her in an evening study. Leeci was excited to join her.

Fay asked Azrael about her growing interest in Bible studies.

"Ma'am, when Theodore told me she had memorized the Holy Bible, I wondered how anyone could do it. I mean, I like could ask her something like 'What is *John 15:13*?' And I had to look up the verse, just to ask the question," she explained. "Without hesitation, Theodore would say, 'Greater love has no one than this: to lay down one's life for one's friends.'"

Fay smiled. "What did you think about what she said?"

"The verse is so true, ma'am," Azrael responded. "It is something I would do. Without hesitation."

"I know you would," Fay said. "It is hardwired into your fiber. Your essence, for lack of a better word. It is why you are a Marine and I think why the angel chose you."

"I have come to realize how much Lady K loves you," Azrael revealed. "She, without hesitation, agreed to trade her life for yours when the angel offered the deal to her."

Tears filled Fay's eyes. While she dabbed the tears away with a tissue, she shared, "I feel that quality within all of us. You, Don, Katrinka, Sasha, Irishka, my sister…you all share a divine relationship."

Don added, "I have always privately felt the same way about all of you."

Azrael admitted, "I have been having interesting dreams of late, guys, where I am meeting with women who are badasses."

"Do you want to share with us, sweetheart?" Fay respectfully inquired.

"I don't mind, ma'am. It's odd. When I talk to them, it's in languages I don't speak, yet I understand our conversations." Azrael had a look of doubt on her face. "Do you know what I mean?"

Winslow said, "I have had dreams like those before. Sometimes I think I don't know this language, yet I am confident in speaking it."

"Yeah! Like that!" Azrael replied.

"Who do you talk to?" Fay was intrigued.

"I talked to that French lady? I forget her name...You know, Don. The warrior?" Azrael guessed.

"Jeanne d'Arc? Winslow guessed.

"Yeah! That's her!" Azrael replied.

"You are conversing in French?" Leeci, who had been listening to the conversation, asked.

"She asks for my advice," Azrael said. "It's French. I don't speak French, but I know what she is saying, Leeci. Crazy, right?"

"Who else?" Fay asked.

"I think she is an English woman? She speaks English but it's a different version than we speak," Azrael replied.

"Is she Boudica?" Winslow asked.

"I don't know. Who is she, Don?"

"Boudica was an English warrior queen," Winslow answered. "She took exception with the Romans. She formed an army and fought with them for England's freedom from Roman oppression. She and her army burned London to the ground, killing tens of thousands Roman soldiers in doing so."

"Geez!" Azrael exclaimed. "And then I talk to Lady K, too."

"What do you and Katrinka talk about?" Fay asked.

"We were, like, in the Louvre…you know…the museum we visited in Paris?"

Fay nodded.

"We were speaking in Russian," Azrael went on. "She asked me how she could best serve the Russian people. It's so crazy. Like, how would I know that stuff? But I had an answer for her."

As Fay listened, she grew concerned. She realized what the source of Azrael's dreams might be. Perhaps when the angel had departed Azrael's soul, she had left behind memories she had had from past meetings with Jeanne d'Arc, Boudica, Katrinka, and others. Those memories were now manifesting in the form of dreams, possibly because of Azrael's new interest in religions and the Bible, which was, in turn, inspired by Theodore's association with Corporal Lopez.

Fay asked, "Azrael, are these dreams disturbing you?"

Azrael had a ready answer for her. "Not at all, ma'am. They are, like, really interesting. And I feel really good when I wake up."

"You seem to be developing an alter-ego, Azrael." Fay smiled. "Promise me if you change your mind about your dreams, you will talk to me about it. I am here for you. Okay?"

"Yes, ma'am."

****

Same day, Moscow, Russia

Another cold, gray, wet morning mirrored her mood. Katrinka watched the rain drops stream down the windowpane of her apartment's living room. The future Grand Duchess of Russia with all the potential, the fame, the riches, was ready to trade it all for the life she had begun but had then been cut short in America: nursing school at the University of Washington, her job and friends at the "Simply Beans Coffeehouse" on the "Ave." She missed her mother, her cat Binky, and she missed Andrew. The princess was angry, sad, and she was most unhappy. But she had made a deal with the Angel of Death, and she was going to honor the bargain without fail until her final day on Earth.

She had always appreciated her confidants, those she now most trusted: her papa Sasha, Faya, and her mentor and life friend Irishka. And there was her Buddy. She could remove the walking boot today. Maybe tomorrow she and Buddy could enjoy a jog around the Kremlin? And then she would kick his ass, as promised. The thought of it drew a chuckle from her heart.

The coffee in her apartment was crap. A famous American coffeehouse was eight hundred meters from her home. For security reasons, she was not allowed to venture beyond the Kremlin walls unescorted. On this day, that which was forbidden, and the rain, would not deter her desire for good coffee. Katrinka pulled on a pair of boots, grabbed a jacket, and set off. About halfway to the coffee house, it occurred to her her raingear would have been complete had she thought to include an umbrella. Or at least a hat. Her hair was sopping wet. No turning back now.

The line at the coffee house was short. While she dug into her pocketbook for a credit card, she glanced at the man standing next to her. "On me," she offered. She then asked, "How?"

"I was coming through the gate, saw you going out. I said 'hello.' You neither saw nor heard me. So, I followed you here," Buddy said.

"Sorry." She apologized. "I have so much on my mind…and I am not happy." She added, "I am not happy, and I am pissed off."

Buddy remained silent, apparently for two legitimate reasons.

The coffees were delivered. Katrinka suggested, "Let's sit by the window." She nodded in the general direction of a corner window located away from the entry door. Years of spy school training had taught her to always sit facing a door. As she sat, she patted the chair next to her. "You must sit next to me," she instructed.

Buddy obliged.

"Old habit," Katrinka said. Her original intent was to sip good coffee and catch a moment or two of personal solace. But Buddy was a good guy. She welcomed his company.

"Can I help?" His voice conveyed concern.

"You can talk to me, my friend. I took my walking boot off today."

"I noticed."

"Tomorrow, you and I are going to run around the Kremlin wall. Outside," Katrinka decided.

"Jog?

"Run. We are going to celebrate my new ankle with good run," she informed him. "Are you ready for it?"

"Always. But are you sure you will be able to keep up with me?" he challenged.

"So…" She toyed with him. "Should we go twice around?"

Buddy laughed and then blew on the top of this

coffee in an attempt to cool it to a tolerable sipping temperature.

Katrinka continued. "When I was in spy school, we would run twice around Kremlin. Sometimes after we had been awakened in early morning after only one hour sleep," she explained. "Somewhere near end, someone would jump out of bush and attack me. Then I had to fight with them." She shook her head as if she were recalling the event. She added, "And I better not lose fight."

Buddy listened in apparent awe.

"So, my dear buddy Buddy," she held his hands in hers she spoke, "I think I am getting soft in old age. So, do not let me get behind you or maybe attack will get you. And then you must fight with me!" Katrinka teased. She spoke frankly when she asked Buddy, "In your opinion, do I look like lady?"

Buddy smiled. "I've known you long enough, Princess, to not insult you that way."

Katrinka laughed. "What I like about you, Buddy Lee. Your honesty is like Faya, it is unfailing. Don't change it."

****

The following morning, while she ate breakfast with Irishka, Katrinka announced her plan for the day. "I am going to run around Kremlin this morning."

"Inside?" Irishka asked.

"No. Outside," Katrinka informed her.

"Why?"

"Because I can," Katrinka answered. "I want to test broken leg."

"You are idiot," Irishka pointed out. "For you to run, you must have security. I am security and I do not

179

want to run." She paused and then said, "And I run better than you." Irishka continued. "For us to run around Kremlin like crazed women, someone from special security force must run too. Who can do it? So then helicopter follows around?"

"I cannot run?" Katrinka asked innocently.

"How about treadmill?" Irishka suggested. "I can read magazine and watch while you run crazy."

"Is not same," Katrinka protested. "What about fresh air?"

"Is no way. No more talk of it," Irishka insisted. "Is final."

An hour later, Buddy, Irishka, and Katrinka exited the main gate nearby dead Lenin's Tomb for their epic run around the Kremlin. And there was a Russian Army helicopter stationed overhead. The distance was to be a mere two miles.

"We run," Katrinka reminded her running partners. "Last one must buy lunch for all at Zhivago."

Buddy and Irishka had both packed their 9mm Markov handguns, giving Katrinka the weight advantage. At around the one-mile mark, Katrinka's leg informed her this running business was not a sound idea. But she pushed through the growing pain and kept up with Buddy and Irishka. Katrinka conceded Irishka's earlier observation. She was an idiot.

Chapter 18

On the bridge of the world's most powerful vessel, a woman with a lot on her mind could process the many thoughts troubling her. The wind never ceased. Her hair, however done, was in an instant now undone. The extreme noise of launching aircraft. The intense activity so choreographed, like a ballet. The danger...how very extreme. It all became her new favorite perch to roost. And it was a place where she could look forward into the future and, in the blink of her eye, look back into the past. She always enjoyed a cup of strong coffee and a quick chat with one of the bridge crew, be it the air boss, the captain, the X-O, or the able seamen. There was always a polite order to the daily business, an atmosphere of respect, and a fundamental organization on a ship's bridge.

The visit to the bridge always seemed to center Fay. Occasionally, she would invite either Don or Azrael to accompany her on one of her adult timeouts. Regardless, she always felt welcomed on the bridge. At the very depth of her visits was a comfort in knowing her dad, a former Naval carrier pilot, was always there. If a girl were ever to dare to dream, her dream would be to one day find herself in command of a U.S. Navy carrier.

Fay returned, refreshed, for the team morning huddle and modeling her newest and now favorite ballcap.

Azrael noticed in an instant. "Ma'am! I love your cap! Explain!"

Fay removed the cap and handed it to Azrael. "I got it from the air boss," she said. "The skull and cross bones have a humorous meaning. It seems when a carrier pilot inadvertently lands on the wrong carrier, they get awarded the ballcap. Humorous humiliation, I think?"

"How the heck do they land on the wrong carrier, ma'am?" Azrael wanted to know.

"They do it, I guess." Fay considered. "But the mini boss told me it's always suspect if they do it by mistake or on purpose."

"Huh," Azrael commented. She seemed as though she was not quite sure if Fay was pulling her leg or not.

Fay focused on a game plan for Leeci and her upcoming judicial proceedings. She explained to Don, Leeci, and Azrael what Leeci's two options were: either an Article Fifteen, or Captain's Mast, or the Article Thirty-one, the court martial. Fay was concerned about the possibility of it being decided that Leeci should endure the non-judicial punishment. The Captain's Mast would be less stringent than the court martial and Fay would have little or no control over the proceedings. The assigned command officer would have total discursion as to Leeci's fate. Often, the assigned officer would have made a decision prior to his, or her, meeting with the offender. The decision would be career-ending, along with a dishonorable discharge from the Navy.

The court martial, while the upper limit of punishment and so more severe, would afford Fay more control over the outcome. Her last defense had resulted in the acquittal of three Marines who had been accused of murdering their wives. The decision of the court to acquit had been the correct one. The judge had not issued punishments to the three Marines, and they had immediately returned to active duty without reduction in rank or discharge from service. If Fay could somehow convince the command officer to opt for the court martial, Leeci would enjoy more options. Military personnel were given an option to decline the Captain's Mast, except for those serving aboard a vessel. Unfortunately, they did not have the option to decline.

Fay's first challenge was to manage the process which would ultimately seal Leeci's fate. The process leading up to and the scheduling of a court martial could take up to a year's time. Her plan was to eventually leave the Navy and join her daughter Katrinka to assist her in the establishment of her principality. Her commitment to Leeci would take precedence. Her hope was if there was to be a court martial, it would be sooner rather than later. In the meantime, she would help Leeci secure a new duty assignment, for her to return to the U.S.S. *Michael* was out of the question.

"Okay," Fay said, "two more orders of business. While we are cooling our jets - I don't know what that means, but it sounds right - it turns out I get to call in a few favors. The Air-boss owed me one. I promised both Azraels a ride in a fighter."

Azrael gasped. "Wow! When?"

"Tomorrow. 1000 hours." Fay had a surprise. She looked at Winslow and Leeci. "Do the two of you want a ride in a fighter?" she offered.

Both could not say yes fast enough.

"How about you, ma'am?" Winslow asked. "You going?"

"Me and flying do not agree with one another," Fay replied. "Y'all go. Take selfies when you are conscious. I will get the idea."

"Thanks, ma'am," all said in unison.

"Good," she said. "The second issue concerns Leeci. Because it may be months before the military justice system gets around to Leeci and her issue and because it is not a good idea to have her return to the *Michael,* she is reassigned temporary duty to the *Reagan.* You will do here what you did there." Fay smiled. "You good with that?" she asked Leeci.

"Thank you, ma'am," Leeci responded. "Considering the options, this is the best I could hope for."

****

The Kremlin, Moscow, Russia

It was around the same time Katrinka began experiencing the growing pain as she ran on her recently broken ankle when she started hearing a song on her headphones. Something about having sympathy for the devil? The message of the song helped her realize although she hoped to find Mazikim, it would be Mazikim finding her. Not the reverse. She reasoned if Mazikim were to find her, it would be near pain, strife, and sorrow. Because of the current political movement in Russia associated with Katrinka assuming the headship, Mazikim, according to the Angel of Death, would be nearby. Katrinka's experience with the two angels who had followed her from Egypt to France served to support her theory. The conflict diamonds entrusted to her would be the bait she needed to lure Mazikim from hiding.

When she told Sasha of her plan, he protested. She explained she would be able to either strike a bargain with the demon or she would kill the demon. Either way, Mazikim would be gone from her life. She would meet Mazikim alone. A reluctant Sasha conceded and gave her the diamonds.

The rain was intermittent, while a moderate wind ruffled the flags atop the Kremlin. Near Saint Basil's Cathedral, the 16th century church built on the order of Ivan the Terrible, there was a head-chopping block. Katrinka reasoned, because the block had at one time been associated with years of human pain and suffering, Mazikim might be lurking nearby. It was on the block she sat, waiting for the demon to find her.

While she waited for the demon who might never show up, a white crow settled under the eve of a nearby building. A white crow! A mist was forming around Red Square. To add to the drama, a man appeared from the gathering mist. He limped as he approached her. His olive drab uniform topped with a red beret cocked on his head to one side suggested he might be an African military man. Katrinka rose from the block to meet him. Her first impulse was to pop the guy. Put him out of his misery and him out of her life. One hand grasped the butt of the 9mm Markov snugly tucked in the waistband of her blue jeans at the small of her back. He was smiling. He exposed both of his hands, suggesting he intended her no harm. Katrinka decided to wait and see what the guy had to say.

The mysterious man was the first to speak. He spoke in Russian. "Greetings, sister," he said.

Katrinka acknowledged him with a cautious, simple nod.

"I am Cardiraxman." His gaze was steady, his smile remaining constant. "I am honored to finally meet you. I've heard so much about you."

Katrinka was not flattered by his words. "We have business, do we not?" she asked.

"I hope so, friend."

Katrinka's gaze surveyed the area behind the man. "You have friends," she confirmed. "I count four."

"As do you, Princess Yekaterina. I count two." He chuckled. His gaze was directed toward the bird. "And a crow."

"I notice you are limping."

"Let me say, I share your pain, Princess."

"You are Mazikim." She did not have to ask. She knew it to be her demon.

"Some call me by that name." The man smiled again. "But today I am Cardiraxman. And, yes, you and I may have business to discuss."

"You are interested in the stones," she said.

"Do you have them?" he asked.

"Yes," Katrinka responded. "What do you offer in exchange?"

"The anger which rages in your heart, my dear sweet girl. And you will never see nor hear from me again. In exchange for the stones."

"And I am to trust you?"

Cardiraxman laughed, "Rather, it is I who need trust you."

"What evil will these stones bring?" Katrinka had to know.

"I do not have favorites, Yekaterina. I only relish in

the conflict they represent," the demon replied.

"How so?"

"There is a war raging within an eastern African nation. The totalitarian regime is set on the systematic elimination of any and all who oppose them. A small rebel force is forming with the intent to oppose and to overthrow the regime. They can succeed, but they are in need weapons. The stones will allow them to accomplish their goal."

"You favor the good side in this rebellion?" Katrinka asked skeptically.

"I only favor rebellion itself," Mazikim clarified. "'Good side' is merely a point of view. Although in this case, many lives will be spared if the rebels can buy weapons with these stones. Many children will be given the chance to live and to grow and rebuild a war-torn nation. But it is their business."

Katrinka considered Mazikim's words only briefly. She reached into the pouch on the front of her hoodie and removed the stones. "Deal," she declared. "And I nevcr scc nor hcar from you again."

"You might say that all of your demons have been exorcised." Mazikim bowed his head. "I humbly remain yours truly, Lady Yekaterina." He then added, "I have something for you, my princess. Beware. A prophecy, if you will. A girl child was born in a village in Bosnia," he warned. "She is now twenty years of age. This girl who will one day realize a dangerous power and a will capable of tearing down all you have built."

He smiled, turned, and walked into the mist, followed by his four henchmen. The white crow emitted but a single "caw," as if to express her approval. Then, with a flap of her wings, she too disappeared into the mist. Katrinka appreciated her vote of confidence.

Buddy and Irishka approached from the opposite direction of the departing men. Irishka asked, "Is deal done?"

"Done," Katrinka said and smiled.

"The woman with whom you spoke was Mazikim?" Buddy asked.

"Woman?" Katrinka responded.

"The woman, dressed in black. With the long white hair," Irishka explained.

The person Katrinka had met with was certainly not the same person Buddy and Irishka had seen. But she understood their confusion. Or was it her confusion? She asked her friends, "The crow was black, yes?"

"Yes, crow was black," Irishka confirmed. "Why? Your color is going blind?"

"What next, your Highness?" Buddy asked.

"Zhivago. We must celebrate!" Katrinka exclaimed. "We have deal. It is not every day girl can dump two billion rubles in one day! My anger is gone..." She tested her broken leg. "And, yes, we can now run to Zhivago."

****

The following day, U.S.S. *Ronald Regan*, South China Sea

Fay returned to her stateroom-office at 10:15 hours. Winslow was the first to notice.

"Ma'am, your finger," he observed.

"What about my finger?"

"The middle finger on your right hand," he replied.

Fay looked at her finger to confirm they were

indeed discussing the same middle finger which had a cast attached to it. "Oh. Yeah," she responded. "I broke it yesterday while you guys were flying."

"How, ma'am?" Azrael asked.

"I'm embarrassed to say," Fay admitted. "Along with all the crap I have taken this morning, when I salute someone, it's like I'm flipping them off! It's humiliating." She then asked, "Will one of you guys take a picture of it so I can text it to JP and Katrinka and get the crap they are going to give me about it over with?"

"I'll do it for you, ma'am," Winslow volunteered.

The photo was taken and transmitted. Fay pointed out the obvious. "I cannot type with this cast screwing things up. I'm wondering…we could use an extra hand here. Pardon the pun." She looked at Leeci. "How about you remain here for a while and help us out?" She then added, "It's a way better offer than the paint or cleaning detail you're going to draw while you are waiting for this to play out."

Leeci smiled. She seemed excited when she agreed. "Of course, ma'am. I will be happy to."

"How was your flight yesterday, Leeci?" Fay inquired.

"Oh, it was great, ma'am. The pilot said I set a record for barfing!" Leeci shook her head. "I used to think once was it. I guess not."

Fay glanced at the other two. "How about you two pirates?" she asked Don and Azrael.

Their sheepish smiles were their only responses.

"Did anyone think to get pictures?" Fay asked.

More sheepish smiles ensued. "Ma'am," Azrael interjected. "We kind of forgot." Her face lit up. "But the pilots took pictures. We can get them from them."

"The pilots," Fay said with doubt in her voice. "I can imagine."

Azrael asked, "I blacked out ma'am for a while. You don't suppose…?"

Fay said, "Yeah. I suppose she enjoyed it too."

"Cool!" Azrael replied. "Ma'am, speaking of Lady K, did you get the video of her running around the Kremlin?"

"I did!"

"You know, ma'am, there is no such word as 'jog' or 'walk fast' in that girl's vocabulary. When she says, 'Let's run,' it seems like twenty miles per hour." Azrael considered things. "Damn, that's frickin' fast! I was on the track team in high school and I can't keep up with Lady K."

"Kat has the legs for it." Fay observed.

"Like you always tell us, ma'am, Charles Darwin once said, 'He who hesitates is lunch.'" Azrael laughed and shook her head. "I love that one. By the way, I should tell you, after I viewed the video that night, I had another dream."

"You mean the dream where you talk to Katrinka in Russian?" Fay asked.

"Yes, ma'am," Azrael admitted. "She was asking me what to do with the conflict diamonds."

"Did you have advice for her?" Fay was curious.

"I did. I told her to give them to that Mazikim chick," Azrael said. "I don't know why, ma'am. But that is what I told her to do."

"Incredible," Fay said. "She did text me. She told me she gave the stones to Mazikim!"

"Who is Mazikim?" Leeci queried.

"She is one of the Devil's mischievous demons. Her job is to cause trouble whenever and wherever," Fay explained.

"Like the song! About having sympathy for Lucifer?" Leeci questioned.

"I guess so?" Azrael replied.

Fay, not wanting the discussion about angels and demons to continue, decided to change the topic, thinking it best to be transparent with her dear and trusted team. "Guys." She paused to collect her thoughts and to think how best to divulge her embarrassing injury. "How did I break my finger?"

Chapter 19

Moscow, Russia

As their time grew shorter and the day of the big event grew closer, the bombings and public demonstrations grew more frequent. There were no injuries. Katrinka had been advised regardless of what or whom, these events were bound to happen.

Buddy and Katrinka viewed the selfies Fay had texted of her broken finger. Buddy remarked, "How did she break it?"

"She said she was angry and punched wall."

Buddy reviewed the photos again. He asked, "Have you ever punched a wall?"

"No. I usually punch bag… and when I was agent, I punched people. But that is it." Katrinka scrolled through more photos. "Do you want to see picture of cat? Is Binky."

Buddy viewed the photos of the cat with interest and then changed the topic of conversation. "We should get back to planning Russia's big day."

"I hope big day will never come," Katrinka protested.

"Yekaterina, the world will know your name!" Buddy predicted.

"I only want simple life." Katrinka reconsidered. "If I can make difference. If but one child's life will be saved. Or if one elder person will know joy and happiness in their final days. Then, yes, it will all be worth it. Then the world can know my name."

****

U.S.S. Ronald Reagan, South China Sea

Azrael, Winslow, and Leeci Chen turned their collective attention toward Fay, anxious to learn how and why Fay had punched the wall.

Fay pointed at the thick metal wall on the door side of their office. "There is a dent in the wall." In her mind, there was a dent in the steel wall, anyway. Super Girl could do it. But Super Fay, no chance. "I sprained my wrist when I punched it."

Azrael was the first to offer sympathy. "We're sorry, ma'am."

"Thank you, darlin'," she said. "The second time I punched it, I broke my finger."

Her three charges all had a look of both horror and doubt etched in their faces. By their count, she had punched the wall twice.

Fay continued to download her embarrassment. "The third time I punched the wall, it really hurt... I cried." Fay clarified, "I never cry. But I did! In retrospect, I now realize I should not have thrown the first punch."

With a sheepish look, Leeci asked, "Why were you angry, ma'am?"

"I knew you would ask. I had gotten a communication from the Seventh Fleet office. Top secret at the time," Fay divulged. "I need a cup."

Not willing to interrupt to Fay's tale, Winslow offered, "Keep going, ma'am. I'll get you a double strong."

193

Fay flashed Don an appreciative smile. "Thank you, Don." She continued. "The call was to inform me that one of the ships in our task force ran aground."

"Wow!" Azrael responded.

"Yeah, wow," Fay replied. "The ship struck an uncharted island. One of those phony Chinese man-made islands."

Don served her coffee. Fay took a sip. "Nice! Just right, Donald."

Don admitted, "Just so you know, I juiced it with your Caffeine Plus. I thought it might help."

"Perfect!" Fay approved. "The grounding is one thing. The other is the island is Chinese territory. And why do I – we - get involved? There is going to be an investigation and there is a raft of Chinese butt-kissing and diplomatic relations on deck. The reason we are now here in the South China Sea is because we strongly contend the building of those bogus islands."

"Ma'am," Azrael asked, "Forgive a dumb landlocked Marine for asking. What are the 'bogus' islands?"

"Oh…no problem," Fay assured her. "China has been building islands on numerous reefs in the South China Sea. These are military installations with airfields. The islands serve to expand their territorial waters, thus allowing them to claim a bigger chunk of the strategic South China Sea."

Winslow added, "Military and shipping lanes are impacted, and the airfields bring the threat of Chinese air reach closer to the Philippines and all of the U.S.-friendly associated South Pacific Island nations."

"The fallout from the investigation will likely end the careers of several of the bridge crew," Fay interjected. "I was angry about it."

Winslow expressed his concern. "It's understandable," he reasoned.

"By default, I am the resident expert when it comes to collisions. Last year I was involved when a U.S. Naval vessel collided with a Russian Naval vessel," Fay explained. "Several of the officers were relieved of their commands. But there was actually a silver lining to the cloud. Captain Alexander Lavrov represented the Russian contingent of the hearing. As you know, we later became friends. It was because of Sasha I met Katrinka. I later adopted her and now she is my daughter."

"In a way, it turned out okay, ma'am," Leeci said.

"In a way," Fay lamented. "My second anger is a selfish one. When we cycle out of our current duty assignment, Azrael and I are to travel to Moscow as guests of the Russian royal family to attend Katrinka's introduction to the people of Russia and Eastern Europe. The investigation could potentially extend the tour until the investigation is resolved."

All were silent as they processed the gravity of the situation.

Fay continued. "Another opportunity may have presented itself. Leeci, as we all know, does speak, read, and write several dialects of the Chinese language. Why, she was valuable in the task force coding center. I reason there is going to be a lot of chatter back and forth between the U.S. and Chinese over this. It will be to our advantage to have an interpreter on our team."

"Is it possible, ma'am?" an exuberant Leeci asked.

"Not only possible, but done, Seaman Chen," Fay replied. "You are now temporarily assigned to JAG

Corps."

A round of clapping broke out. "Welcome, welcome, welcome," Azrael offered, along with a generous hug for her new friend Leeci.

Fay let the celebration subside. She next added, "If we work hard as a team and if we can put this to bed and still get out of here in time for Azrael and I to get off to Moscow, I will make a deal with all of you. If Don and Leeci would like to travel with us to the celebration in Moscow, I will pay for all expenses. So let me know if and when this works out."

"Thank you, ma'am. I, for one, would be interested." Don had an idea. "I think you might have already thought of this, ma'am, but it seems to me if you wore your parade gloves, your finger would disappear."

"I thought of it, Don. Sadly," Fay replied, "my gloves are not large enough."

Don looked at his hands. "My hands are larger than yours. I will get mine for you."

"Great idea!" Fay approved. "Teamwork! I love it!" she exclaimed.

****

Certain unfortunate occurrences were limited and almost nonexistent in today's military, yet they did occur from time to time. Fay and Azrael were walking from lunch on their way to their office. Azrael was a near six feet tall Marine with an athletic build, while Fay was some two inches shorter and fifteen years her senior. Fay had her right hand on the back of Azrael's near left shoulder. She leaned closer toward Azrael to whisper confidential information. As Fay spoke, they passed by six crewmembers. All presented the requisite salute. Salutes were returned and as Fay passed the group on her left, she heard a whisper. "Lesbian."

A chill passed through her body. She was not aware if Azrael had heard the comment or not. Regardless, the comment warranted revisiting. "HOLD UP!" Fay ordered. She and Azrael retraced their steps to face the six sailors waiting for them, standing at attention.

Fay and Azrael stood to face them. Azrael's time spent in the Embassy Security detail had etched a certain measure of sternness in her dark, desert tanned skin. She was an intimidating woman with the heart of an angel.

Fay spoke. "I think I heard what I think I heard. I hope I did not hear it. Certainly not from six of our own. If you are all on duty, then I won't delay you. I will, however, remind all of you our Navy has several policies which I strongly support as your Commander. Diversity and inclusion. We are a diverse unit. We have dedicated our being to ensure each and every servicemember who serves our country recognizes through inclusion we are a better military and stronger nation for our team efforts." Fay looked each sailor directly in the eyes. She knew Azrael had joined her with a stern Marine glare. Fay finished with, "A word to the wise should be sufficient." She paused for a moment to let her advice sink in. "DISMISSED!" she barked.

Fay and Azrael turned and continued on their intended path.

"That gave me goosebumps, ma'am," Azrael said. "Thank you."

The investigation of the grounding lasted five

weeks. A panel consisting of officers from Seventh Fleet and Fay concluded the crew was accountable. Discharges were deemed appropriate. Fay was able to persuade the panel the discharges should be honorable. She was disappointed the captain and XO's careers were ended, yet she was satisfied her recommendation for the honorable discharge was upheld.

****

Ritz Carlton Moscow

Fay and her entourage arrived at the Ritz three days prior to the gala event. Fay, her sister JP, and Azrael were busy preparing Katrinka for her grand introduction. The entire preparation was as if Katrinka were getting married. What to wear? Makeup and hair? Music? Food? There was electricity in the air. The hotel staff, from catering to room service to the front staff, and the resultants and bars, were all full of anticipation and excitement.

Katrinka was excited to learn her uncle, Prince Eugen, and his wife had requested an audience with Princess Yekaterina two hours prior to the event. Katrinka had not yet met her uncle and aunt, and they had not been aware their niece was even alive until recently. She was to meet them in the Ritz's Presidential Suite at noon. Fay, Azrael, Sasha, Buddy, and Irishka accompanied Kat to the suite.

A lot of thought was devoted to the message which would be sent by Katrinka's clothing style and colors. Buddy had met with Prince Eugen's staff to learn what he and his wife had planned for their wardrobe. Prince Eugen had chosen to wear a gray sport coat, dark slacks, and a white shirt without tie - traditional casual Russian male attire. His wife, Svetlana, chose to wear a traditional eastern European peasant dress, done in lively red, white, and blue colors. Katrinka thought this seemed appropriate and sent the right message. She decided on a colorful peasant maxi-dress to compliment her aunt. The dress was tied at the waist with a rope...ala Jeanne d'Arc. Azrael offered her Tiffany's necklace as a perfect accent to the dress's U-neck design. Irishka wove a red, white, and blue ribbon into Katrinka's hair.

Katrinka and her group had taken rooms at the Ritz as well. Fay sensed in Katrinka a mood much like that of a child on Christmas morning. The prince was her only blood relative. Why had he asked to meet her? The meeting was to be private. Only Katrinka's uncle and aunt were to attend. Irishka would escort Katrinka to the room and remain in the hall accessing the suite with Prince Eugen's security staff.

Fay waited in the hotel lobby with apprehension while the meeting proceeded. Then a hotel manager approached Fay with a message from Katrinka. "Commander Green, Princess Yekaterina would like you and your party to join her in the Presidential Suite," he explained.

Sasha, Fay, Buddy, and Azrael made their way to the hotel's private elevator, which would take them to the suite. Irishka greeted them when they arrived at the room. She knocked on the door. Katrinka opened the door. Fay was taken aback by the joy and exuberance Katrinka exuded. Apparently, the meeting had gone well.

Fay, Sasha, Buddy, and Azrael entered the room. Although invited in, Irishka declined the offer and remained in the hallway. When Katrinka realized

Irishka had declined, she went to the hallway. Several minutes later, Katrinka returned to the room with Irishka. Katrinka then led her guests into a larger room to meet her uncle and aunt.

On seeing the prince and his wife, Fay was floored. Nothing could have prepared her for what she was experiencing. There was another person in the room. As Fay looked from face to face, it was evident to her, they were all, with the exception of Prince Eugen's wife, related. Who was the other person?

Katrinka began the introductions with Fay. Her first introduction was to the prince. A very dashing fellow. He took her hand as Katrinka introduced Fay as her mother. Prince Eugen bowed at the waist and kissed Fay's hand. Because of her adopted association to the princess, Fay reasoned she must have gained a royal title of some sort. Sasha had mentioned to her she could be Princess Mother. He was not sure, however.

When she was introduced to Fay, the prince's wife offered a mild curtsey with a certain air of reverence. Fay, not knowing protocol, retuned her kind greeting with a polite Anjali Mudrā. The next introduction was a shocker. Fay wondered how Katrinka had felt when she had first met her.

"Faya," Katrinka announced, "please meet my sister, Eleonore!" Katrinka placed her face near to Eleonore's. "You see, Faya. We are twin! She is ballet dancer!"

Sasha must have sensed it. He came to Fay's side. His firm hand steadied her left arm. Surely, she would not faint this day?

Sasha, Buddy, and Azrael were also introduced by. Fay was left to wonder why Irishka stood aside and was not included in the family introductions. And yet, she was smiling. Irishka did not often smile. Everyone was asked to sit. Katrinka had an announcement to make.

"I am so happy," she began. "All of my family is here! I did not know I had!" She looked around the room. "I have uncles and aunts. And I have fathers and sisters." Katrinka turned her attention to Fay. "And mother." Her smile was beyond electric. "I do not believe it!" Her excitement began to temper. "I have important news." She turned her attention to Uncle Eugen and Aunt Svetlana. "My uncle and aunt have changed mind. They have asked me if I would agree to allow them to take headship of family Romanov for political and business." Katrinka paused. "I have agreed…"

Applause filled the room. Katrinka waited for the applause to quiet. She raised a glass. "A toast!" All in the room responded. "Long live Prince Eugen and Princess Svetlana," she announced. She paused again. When she had the attention of the room, she continued, "But there is condition. I must assume what will be face of family for public relations purpose. When needed," she added. "And I must assume health and welfare duties for family as well."

Hearing this, Fay must have unconsciously expressed a measure of doubt. "This will be good, Faya. Not to worry about it," Katrinka assured her.

Katrinka asked Azrael if she would take a Romanov family photo. Azrael obliged. Fay thought it odd while Katrinka asked Irishka to again join, she declined. Fay thought it curious. She had often thought Katrinka and Irishka strongly resembled one another. They had the same approximate height and hair color.

Katrinka had never offered an explanation for the two's strong resemblance nor had Fay ever asked. Fay could not hear the discussion which ensued between Katrinka, Eugen, and Irishka. Eventually, Irishka relinquished and joined the family for the photo. Fay was left to wonder was Irishka perhaps Eugen's sister? Katrinka's aunt? She was too young to be Katrinka's mother, yet could well be an older sister. The answer to the question would remain a future mystery to be solved another time.

About an hour later, the new House of Romanoff were introduced to the Russian media, the people of Russia, and to the world. Great pains had been taken to clearly establish the Romanov family were not associated with nor puppets of the Russian government in any way.

Fay could not help but laugh. At some point during the reception following the introduction of the new Romanov family to Russia, and the world, Fay spotted Inspector Popov chatting and laughing with a gala guest. Fay wondered why Katrinka may have included him on her guest list. Perhaps she felt she needed to clear the air with their pal Apple Cheeks? He may have had both she and Katrinka still on his list of suspects related to the assassinations of Evilenko and Roman Justine. What Fay did not notice at first glance was who Inspector Popov was conversing with. The man was somewhat thinner in both hair and build, but it was him. She added her old friend Gifford to her must-meet list.

Finally, she managed to break free from those who wanted a word and worked her way through the crowd. "Gifford!" she shrieked and hugged the man she had shared so many adventures with. The NCC journalist who had lent his journalistic skills to help her finish her father's memoirs and the CIA agent who had led her to and ultimately had helped her bring to justice the Galaxy Friendship Association in one of the nation's largest anti-trust cases in recent memory.

Gifford held Fay a while longer and then released her. He stepped back to admire her. "You are more beautiful than I last remember. How have you been, my dear friend?"

"Better than anyone, Champion!" Fay hugged him again. "And how has my favorite spook been?"

"Alive and kicking, as they say."

Fay was radiant. "How? Why are you here?"

"Lady Yekaterina invited me. And I am to cover the event for my employer, NCC."

"Oh. My dear, dear friend. How long will you be in town? Will we have time to have dinner? So very much has happened since we last met. I will not take 'no' for an answer," Fay urged.

"I am scheduled to fly out tomorrow," Gifford admitted. He acquiesced. "But if you insist, I will stay on."

"I insist. Even if I have to tie you to a chair," Fay kidded. "We will match schedules." Fay began to walk away. She stopped, turned, and said, "You have to meet my daughter. She is to die for."

****

Later in the evening, Fay met Gifford Champion for a late dinner at her go-to favorite dinning spot in Moscow, the Grande Café Dr. Zhivago, across from the Kremlin. For Fay, it was an unexpected and wonderful reunion with one of her dearest friends. It had been so long since their last meeting and there was so much to catch up on. About an hour into the dinner, Fay received a text. She excused herself and clicked on her phone. "It's Kat," she informed Gifford. "She and her guy Andrew are out on the town. She is checking in."

Gifford smiled with delight. "Is she near? Can she join us?"

"Is it okay with you, Gifford?" Fay wondered.

"I would be humbled to meet Russia's new princess."

Fay turned her attention back to her cell. "Honey, why don't you and Andrew meet my friend and I at Zhivago's?" she said to Kat.

"Okay, mama," Kat replied. "We can be there fifteen minutes. *Paca paca.*"

"See you." Fay clicked off.

"Andrew?" Gifford asked. "I know the name. Don't I?"

"Yes. You do," Fay responded. "Think back to our op in South Korea and my episode when I visited the U.S.S. *Johnathan Carr.*"

Gifford thought for a brief moment. "Yes! Of course!" he exclaimed. "The Navy SEAL who rescued you when you were stranded in the Yellow Sea."

"Yes," Fay corroborated.

"And he has somehow met Lady Yekaterina?"

"I had a hand in it."

"I am sure you did!" Gifford confirmed.

Shortly after, Katrinka and Andrew entered. Fay had not had a chance to reacquaint herself with Andrew for almost one year. She rose and embraced the unassuming and handsome Navy SEAL. "Andrew, I am always happy to see you."

"Good to see you, ma'am," he responded.

"Fay," she reminded him.

Andrew acknowledged this with a nod and a smile.

Fay made the introductions. "Andrew and Kat, I want you to meet my dearest friend, Gifford Champion."

Gifford also rose. He offered his hand to both of the new guests. "Please, all welcome. Please sit," he offered.

Drinks were ordered, followed by a lively conversation. Katrinka asked, "Mr. Champion, my mama has told me so many stories over the time about you and her, I have grown to feel as if I know you. And, sir, I have the deepest respect for your wisdom and knowledge. May I ask your opinion?" she hesitantly asked.

"I would be honored," Gifford replied.

Katrinka adjusted herself in her chair as if she were organizing her thoughts. "Mr. Champion, I have a good problem, I think? Anyway, I have inherited maybe more than ninety million U.S. dollars. I do not want this money. It is not me. I know Faya will have much good advice for me and I would like to ask your opinion as well."

"You would like to donate this money to a charity?" Gifford guessed.

"Yes, if it is how to do it. Thank you," Katrinka responded. "I am only twenty-five-year-old girl. I don't know about these things."

"Thank you for asking, princess. It can be a problem, for sure. And it will take much thought and discussion. But I am willing to offer an idea," Gifford answered.

"Please," Katrinka responded.

"Your mother has told me you wish to help children and you are concerned about the welfare of your fellow man as well."

Katrinka eagerly nodded, yes.

"UNICEF is an international charity set up to save children's lives. They are designed to fight for children's rights and provide may opportunities needed to give children an equitable chance in life," Gifford informed her.

"And you and Faya will help me to contact this UNICEF charity?"

"We will," Fay assured her. She asked Gifford, "Through your connections, would there be an opportunity for Katrinka at the World Bank?"

Gifford's eyes brightened. "Good idea! Yes, I think so!"

Fay said, "The World Bank is set up to fight poverty on a worldwide scope, among many other things."

Katrinka said, "It sounds good to me. I give to them this money and only good things can happen." She paused. "And no mafia to steal it?"

All laughed. "No mafia, darlin', I promise," Fay assured her.

"Okay. We can meet with them. I think one third of this money to Bank. One third to UNICEF, and...mama?"

"Yes, honey?" Fay prompted.

"You know hospital I visit near university. Children's Hospital. I think they need this money too. So, one third. And I can keep some millions." Katrinka looked at Andrew. "I am sorry, sweet. I hate to say it, but your car is the crap car. I need some money to buy you better car." She hesitated. "But not new car!" she proclaimed.

Again, more laughter ensued.

While the conversation and planning continued, Fay wondered how the turn of events which had placed Prince Eugen in the headship of the royal family might affect Katrinka's bargain with the archangel Azrael. Was their deal now null and void?

Fay's concern was satisfied when she noticed Katrinka's distraction. Fay followed Katrinka's line of sight to a nearby window. There on the sill perched a great white raven. Katrinka's lips were moving as if she were whispering to the bird. The bird then seemed to turn her attention to Fay. Next, the white raven spread her mighty wings. The bird held them expanded for a moment, reminding Fay of the recent meeting in the Paris courtyard where the archangel had spread her wings. She cawed, one time, as if she were voicing her approval. With a flap of her wings, the raven launched from her perch and flew away.

A word about the author...

Except for time spent in military service I live in the Pacific Northwest with my legal-beagle son K-K. and seven large tropical fish from the Amazon River. I am a second-generation Seattleite (that's what they call those of us who dwell in the shadow of Mr. Rainier). I have had the opportunity to travel our planet many times over. My stories are created from my memories of my personal experiences, the places I have visited, and the people and friends I have known.